KINGSLEY JUNIOR HIGH SCHOOL

The Cuban Americans

IMMIGRANTS IN AMERICA

The Cuban Americans

Other books in the Immigrants in America series:

The Chinese Americans
The Italian Americans
The Russian Americans
The Vietnamese Americans

IMMIGRANTS IN AMERICA

The Cuban Americans

By Liz Sonneborn

10911 Technology Place, San Diego, CA 92127
McLean County Unit #5
204-Kingsley

Library of Congress Cataloging-in-Publication Data

Sonneborn, Elizabeth.
　　The Cuban Americans / by Elizabeth Sonneborn.
　　　　p. cm. — (Immigrants in America)
　　Includes bibliographical references and index.
　　Summary: Discusses the past and present political upheavals that drove the Cubans to American soil and their ultimate success.
　　　ISBN 1-56006-902-3 (hardback: alk. paper)
　　　1. Cuban Americans—History—Juvenile literature. 2. Cuba—Emigration and immigration—History—Juvenile literature. 3. United States—Emigration and immigration—History—Juvenile literature. 4. Cuba—History—Juvenile literature.
　　[1. Cuban Americans—History. 2. Cuba—Emigration and immigration—History. 3. United States—Emigration and immigration—History. 4. Cuba—History.] I. Title. II. Series.
　　　E184.C97 S66 2002
　　　973'.04687291—dc21
2001005774

Copyright © 2002 by Lucent Books, Inc.
10911 Technology Place, San Diego, CA 92127

No part of this book may be reproduced or used in any form or by any means, electrical, mechanical, or otherwise, including, but not limited to, photocopy, recording, or any information storage and retrieval system, without prior permission from the publisher.

Printed in the U.S.A.

Contents

Foreword	6
Introduction	
The Cuban American Success Story	8
Chapter One	
Between Two Worlds	12
Chapter Two	
Escaping Castro	24
Chapter Three	
The Golden Exiles	37
Chapter Four	
Blending Old and New	50
Chapter Five	
Becoming Cuban American	62
Chapter Six	
The Marielitos	74
Chapter Seven	
Elian and Beyond	86
Notes	99
For Further Reading	102
Works Consulted	103
Index	106
Picture Credits	111
About the Author	112

Foreword

Immigrants have come to America at different times, for different reasons, and from many different places. They leave their homelands to escape religious and political persecution, poverty, war, famine, and countless other hardships. The journey is rarely easy. Sometimes, it entails a long and hazardous ocean voyage. Other times, it follows a circuitous route through refugee camps and foreign countries. At the turn of the twentieth century, for instance, Italian peasants, fleeing poverty, boarded steamships bound for New York, Boston, and other eastern seaports. And during the 1970s and 1980s, Vietnamese men, women, and children, victims of a devastating war, began arriving at refugee camps in Arkansas, Pennsylvania, Florida, and California, en route to establishing new lives in the United States.

Whatever the circumstances surrounding their departure, the immigrants' journey is always made more difficult by the knowledge that they leave behind family, friends, and a familiar way of life. Despite this, immigrants continue to come to America because, for many, the United States represents something they could not find at home: freedom and opportunity for themselves and their children.

No matter what their reasons for emigrating, where they have come from, or when they left, once here, nearly all immigrants face considerable challenges in adapting and making the United States their new home. Language barriers, unfamiliar surroundings, and sometimes hostile neighbors make it difficult for immigrants to assimilate into American society. Some Vietnamese, for instance, could not read or write in their native tongue when they arrived in the United States. This heightened their struggle to communicate with employers who demanded they be literate in English, a language vastly different from their own. Likewise, Irish immigrant school children in Boston faced classmates who teased and belittled their lilting accent. Immigrants from Russia often felt isolated, having settled in areas of the United States where they had no access to traditional Russian foods. Similarly, Italian families, used to certain wines and spices, rarely shopped or traveled outside of New York's Little Italy, a self-contained community cut off from the rest of the city.

Even when first-generation immigrants do successfully settle into life in the United States, their children, born in America, often have different values and are influenced more by their country of birth than their parents' traditions. Children want to be a part of the American culture and usually welcome American ideals, beliefs, and styles. As they become more Americanized—adopting western dating habits and fashions, for instance—they tend to cast aside or even actively reject the traditions embraced by their parents. Assimilation, then, often becomes an ideological dispute that creates conflict among immigrants of every ethnicity. Whether Chinese, Italian, Russian, or Vietnamese, young people battle their elders for respect, individuality, and freedom, issues that often would not have come up in their homeland. And no matter how tightly the first generations hold onto their traditions, in the end, it is usually the young people who decide what to keep and what to discard.

The Immigrants in America series fully examines the immigrant experience. Each book in the series discusses why the immigrants left their homeland, what the journey to America was like, what they experienced when they arrived, and the challenges of assimilation. Each volume includes discussion of triumph and tragedy, contributions and influences, history and the future. Fully documented primary and secondary source quotations enliven the text. Sidebars highlight interesting events and personalities. Annotated bibliographies offer ideas for additional research. Each book in this dynamic series provides students with a wealth of information as well as launching points for further discussion.

INTRODUCTION

The Cuban American Success Story

Before the mid–twentieth century, few Cubans moved to the United States to live permanently. There were exceptions, of course: generally political radicals, who fled north in search of a safe haven from persecution. By far, the majority of Cubans arriving in America were tourists, students, or workers, most of whom viewed their stay in the United States as temporary. In their minds, no matter how long they stayed, Cuba remained their home, and they planned to return there one day.

This pattern abruptly changed in 1959—the year Fidel Castro took over as Cuba's leader. Almost immediately, thousands of Cubans fled the island, many to avoid facing Castro's firing squads. Most of these emigrants headed to the United States, and by 1962 the population of Cubans in the United States had risen from 20,000 in the pre-Castro era to more than 250,000. And this was only the first wave of Cuban emigration. Eventually more than 1 million Cubans—10 percent of the country's population—would leave the island and head for new lives in the United States.

The speed and scope of their immigration sets the experience of Cuban Americans apart from that of other immigrants, but it is only one of several ways their experience differs. Most obvious, they differ from other American immigrant groups in the decision many Cubans made to settle in one geographical area. Whereas the population of most immigrant groups spreads out geographically over time, the Cuban Americans have become more concentrated. Of the 1.3 million people of Cuban heritage in the United States today, two out of three live in Florida.

From the beginning, Cubans flocked to southern Florida, particularly Miami, because of its proximity to Cuba. The first immigrants to arrive after Castro's rise to power expected that he would soon be overthrown. In that event, they wanted to be close to Cuba so they could return home quickly. As these Cubans set down roots in Miami, their presence attracted newcomers to the city because of the Cuban flavor of "Little Havana," the neighborhood where the first immigrants had settled. By the 1970s, Cuban Americans who had initially moved to other areas began relocating to Miami just to experience Little Havana's sights and sounds.

Cuban Americans are also unusual in the financial success they have achieved. The first immigrants were nicknamed "the Golden Exiles"—an acknowledgment of the wealth and high social standing they had enjoyed in Cuba. When they left the country, their wealth was confiscated by the Castro regime, leaving them penniless as they arrived in the United States. Nevertheless,

In search of freedom, Cuban refugees land a crowded boat off the coast of Florida.

their level of education and the business experience allowed them to prosper in the United States. The emergence of Miami from a small resort town to a cosmopolitan metropolis has been attributed in large part to the entrepreneurial drive and expertise of these early Cuban immigrants.

Unlike many other immigrant groups, Cuban Americans have also strongly resisted the idea that they might never return to their homeland. The majority of Cuban Americans, especially those in the first waves who left Cuba in the 1960s, did so almost purely for political reasons. They had little desire or incentive to shed their identity as Cubans. As Cuban American attorney Luis Botifoll has explained: "[Most] immigrants want to assimilate because, by and large, they have brought with them unhappy memories of their native countries. But we don't have bad memories of Cuba. Before 1959, we did not think the U.S. was better. We thought *Cuba* was better. And most of us still do."[1]

This passion for their homeland continues to be a powerful force in the lives of many Cuban Americans. It is most evident in their continuing interest in contemporary developments in Cuba. Even for those who have spent decades in the United States, keeping up with Cuban politics is a part of daily life. Many are also involved in Cuban American

A strong work ethic has allowed Cuban Americans to prosper in the United States.

political groups dedicated to influencing the U.S. policies toward Castro. Their involvement in these issues makes Cuban Americans the most politically active immigrant group in the United States today.

The powerful role their homeland still plays in their imagination also distinguishes Cuban Americans. For many Cuban Americans, especially those of the older generations, memories of Cuba are cherished and preserved. Writing in 1998, scholar Miguel Gonzalez-Pando explained the power of these memories: "Together with more than a million fellow emigrés who make up the Cuban diaspora, I live outside of Cuba but still consider myself part of that nation. I yearn for its azure waters, cooling breezes and the smell that lingered in my home's backyard after a thunderstorm."[2]

Similar memories inspire large numbers of Cuban Americans to dream of one day returning to Cuba when Castro is no longer its leader. For them, being Cuban American means having a dual identity. They may be American in the here and now. But, remembering their past, they look forward to a future when they can once again be Cuban.

CHAPTER ONE

Between Two Worlds

"I never beheld so fair a thing; trees all along the river, beautiful and green and different from ours, with flowers and fruits each according to their kind, and little birds which sing very sweetly."[3] Explorer Christopher Columbus wrote these words in his journal on October 28, 1492, while traveling across the island of Cuba. Columbus's expedition was funded by the king and queen of Spain, and he claimed possession of the island on their behalf. As a result, Spain considered Cuba to be its colony for more than four hundred years.

By the eighteenth century, however, many Cubans were eager to shake Spanish rule. As they began thinking of themselves more as Cubans than as Spaniards, they wanted to establish their own government and control their own destiny.

For Cubans, the road to independence was long and full of many twists and turns. One complication was the presence of a second foreign power—the United States—that increasingly tried to exert its influence over Cuba and its people. As a safe haven for Cuban political exiles, the United States in many ways seemed to be a friend to those who dreamed of a Cuba free of Spanish rule. But during the nineteenth century, growing American interference in Cuban affairs alarmed Cubans, convincing them that Americans were no less threatening to Cuban freedom than their Spanish oppressors.

The Spanish in Cuba

Few Spaniards visited Cuba until 1511, when adventurer Diego Velázquez led an army of soldiers to the island. At the time, Cuba was inhabited by about one hundred thousand Indians of the Guanahatabey, Ciboney, and Taino tribes. The Spanish quickly took control of Cuba and enslaved these peoples. Even worse for the Indians, the Spanish brought with them new diseases such as measles and smallpox. Because the Indians had no natural immunities to these diseases, they died in large numbers. Within fifty years, the Indian population of Cuba dropped to fewer than five thousand.

The near extinction of Cuba's indigenous peoples soon presented the Spanish with a problem. In the seventeenth century, the Spanish in Cuba began growing sugar and tobacco and raising cattle. As the Indians died off, finding laborers to work on these farms was difficult. To overcome the labor shortage, the *criollos*—people of Spanish and Indian descent who owned many of the farms—began importing slaves from Africa to work their land.

The decision to import slaves was to have a lasting impact on Cuban society. Unlike

Europeans purchase sugar from the Indians of Cuba.

BETWEEN TWO WORLDS 13

slaves in most areas of North America, Cuban slaves were often eventually allowed to buy or negotiate their own freedom. Over time, there grew up a class of free blacks who worked as artisans or who operated their own small farms and ranches. This group, along with the *criollos,* eventually came to comprise the two largest ethnic groups in Cuba.

Although many *criollos* grew wealthy from their businesses, they resented the way they were treated by Spain. Important government positions were given to Spaniards. The *criollos* were also angered by Spanish trade regulations. For example, the Spanish monarchs dictated that the Cubans could sell tobacco only to them at low prices set by the Crown. The Spanish Crown then resold the tobacco at a huge profit.

Coming to America

Responding to the frustrations of the *criollos,* Spain loosened the rules on Cuban trade in the 1770s, allowing its colony to trade with other nations. Soon, one of Cuba's most important trading partners was the United States. Cuban merchants began making regular business trips to New York, Philadelphia, and New Orleans. Contact between Cubans and Americans grew even more common after 1819, when Spain sold Florida to the United States. With only a 90-mile strip of water—the Straits of Florida—separating Cuba from Florida's southernmost tip, Cubans began doing more and more business with their American neighbors.

Some Cubans visited the United States for trading purposes. Others found sanctuary there when their political views put them at odds with Spain's colonial authorities. One of the first Cuban political exiles was Father Felix Varela y Morales. Varela was a Catholic priest who had earned a reputation in Cuba as a brilliant scholar. Varela was also a dynamic and persuasive orator, and he made himself unpopular with the Spanish government with his public demands for the abolition of slavery in Cuba and his call for reforms in the Catholic Church. Most disturbing of all to colonial authorities, Varela made no secret of his belief that Cuba should break away from Spain and become an independent country.

Fearing for his life, Varela in 1821 fled to New York City. Gradually, over the next thirty years, other Cubans who held similar views also migrated to New York, and Varela became a leader of this exiled community. To promote Cuban independence, he published a newspaper, *El Habanero*. (The title meant "a person from Havana," Cuba's largest city.) Varela saw to it that copies of *El Habanero* were smuggled into Cuba. Threatened by the revolutionary spirit Varela was stirring up, Spain's colonial government sent an assassin to New York to kill him. The plot misfired, however; Varela confronted his would-be killer and, using his considerable power of persuasion, convinced the assassin to let him live.

By the 1840s, many *criollos* shared Varela's desire to see Cuba free of Spanish control. But instead of wanting an independent Cuba, they wanted their country to become part of the United States. The *criollos* did so much business with the United States that Cuba's becoming part of America would work to their financial advantage by strengthening their ties to American businesses. The *criollos* were inspired in their efforts by the example of Texas, which had rebelled against Mexico, and after a brief period of independence had agreed to join the United States. The *criollos* thought that if they could set off a similar rebellion in Cuba, the United States would eventually annex Cuba just as it had Texas. With this idea in mind, on three separate occasions, in 1848, 1849, and 1851, a *criollo*-funded organization located in the United States known as Club de la Habana (The Havana Club) sent small-scale military expeditions into Cuba. The organization hoped that the troops, led by Narciso López into Cuba, would incite a popular revolt. However, few Cubans joined the fight. Eventually, López was captured and executed by the Spanish.

Following The Havana Club's unsuccessful attempts at inciting rebellion, the *criollos* tried a different tactic: They used their influence with American businesspeople to push the United States to purchase Cuba from Spain. These Americans succeeded in convincing political leaders in the United States that Cuba should be acquired, but despite two different offers from the United States, Spain refused to sell. Through various land sales and independence movements, Spain had already lost nearly all the possessions it had once claimed in the Americas. As a result, Cuba emerged as Spain's most important and profitable colony, and the Spanish were not eager to let it go.

A sign announces a rally condemning the Spanish occupation of Cuba.

The Ten Years' War

The *criollos*, however, persisted in their drive to break away from Spain. On October 10, 1868, a group of *criollo* sugar planters and cattle ranchers met in the town of Yara, Cuba. There, led by planter Carlos Manuel de Céspedes, they drafted a constitution and declared that their homeland was now the free and independent Republic of Cuba.

By this time, it was clear to many Cubans that the Spanish government would never willingly give up its control of the island. The only way they would gain their freedom was by fighting for it. As Spanish soldiers rushed to quell Céspedes's revolt, he found a large number of recruits for his rebel force. Within a month, he had fifteen thousand supporters. This force included both disgruntled *criollos* and poor blacks, whom the Spanish had often treated brutally. Using

Cuban rebels burn a sugar cane plantation during the Ten Years' War.

guerrilla tactics, Céspedes and his followers continued fighting for nearly a decade, earning the bloody conflict the name the Ten Years' War.

The war uprooted large numbers of Cubans, thousands of whom fled to safety in New York, New Orleans, and other American cities. In the 1870s, the number of Cubans living in the United States more than doubled, rising to more than ten thousand. These immigrants did not view their move to the United States as permanent, however. In fact, many devoted themselves to helping the rebels win the war in hopes that they could one day return home to an independent Cuba. They founded several organizations to aid the war effort, including Instituto San Carlos (San Carlos Institute) in Key West, Florida. These organizations provided both financial aid and moral support to the rebellion leaders.

Despite the support of the exiled Cubans, the rebellion failed. Worn down by the war, rebellion leaders began fighting among themselves. The leadership became even more disordered after Céspedes was ambushed and killed by Spanish troops in 1874. Four years later, the rebels admitted defeat and agreed to stop the fighting.

The Ten Years' War was over, but its effects were felt for decades. More than two hundred thousand people had been killed during the war, and many plantations had been destroyed. As a result, the Cuban economy was in shambles. Many *criollos* went bankrupt. The U.S. consul in Havana reported that "out of the twelve or thirteen hundred planters on the island, not a dozen are said to be solvent."[4] Most had no choice but to sell their land, and American businesspeople, seeing an opportunity to make a potentially lucrative investment, bought the plantations, tying Cuba's economy even more closely to that of the United States.

Cigar City

With the Cuban economy wrecked, little work could be found in Cuba. Some Cuban laborers had no choice but to move to the United States, where jobs were plentiful in cigar factories. These cigar factories were established by Cubans during the mid–nineteenth century. Before that time, owners of cigar factories in Cuba had exported much of their product to the United States. But in the 1870s, the U.S. government began imposing high taxes on cigars imported from Cuba. These taxes made it too expensive for Cuban cigar makers to sell their goods in America. Many Cuban cigar makers soon realized they could avoid paying these import taxes if they manufactured their cigars on U.S. soil. To continue to tap the lucrative U.S.

Paulina Pedroso

Central to the Cuban independence movement was Paulina Pedroso, a Cuban woman of African descent. After the Cubans' defeat in the Ten Years' War in 1878, she and her husband Ruperto settled in Key West, Florida. In the 1880s the Pedrosos moved to Ybor City on the outskirts of Tampa. Ruperto found work in one of the many cigar factories in the town. Paulina ran a boarding house that catered to young Cuban men who came to Ybor City to find jobs.

A frequent visitor to her boarding house was the Cuban leader José Martí. As he planned a Cuban revolution, he often came to Ybor City to garner the support of the cigar workers there. Whenever he came to town, Paulina Pedroso flew a Cuban flag outside her boarding house. Cuban workers then flocked around the building, hoping to catch a glimpse of the great revolutionary.

Pedroso worked tirelessly for the Partido Revolucionario Cubano, a political organization founded by Martí. She and her husband even sold their house to help finance the revolution. After the Cuban rebels' victory, she was highly involved in La Unión Martí-Maceo, an organization founded to help black Cubans. It was named after Martí and the black Cuban general Antonio Maceo, both of whom died while fighting the revolution.

In 1910 Paulina Pedroso returned to Cuba. Until her death in 1925, she was honored as a hero. The site of her Ybor City house, now a park, features a plaque that reads PAULINA PEDROSO WAS ONE OF THE GREAT WOMEN PATRIOTS OF CUBA.

Reading to the Workers

Cuban cigar workers retained a workplace custom from their homeland. They hired a lector *(reader) who sat at a* tribuna *(platform) in the middle of the factory floor. While they worked, the* lector *read aloud from books, magazines, and newspapers. The workers voted on what the* lector *would read. They often wanted to hear novels and stories, but they also insisted the* lector *read Cuban newspapers, political works, and publications produced by labor unions.*

In an interview with historian Louis A. Pérez Jr., published in the Fall/Winter, 1985, Tampa Bay History, *Abelardo Gutiérrez Diaz, a Cuban cigar worker in the 1920s, gave this description of the skills needed to be a successful* lector.

One had to read with feeling. More than anything else, one had to act out his material.... He had to breathe life into his protagonists. The old lady—the old man: when they argued, when they yelled. All that. You know, it was not all that easy.

And quite naturally, there were favorite *lectores.* Some *lectores* were sought after more than others. There was often competition among factories to secure the service of a particularly gifted *lector.* . . . There was one case of a *lector* who did not have a powerful voice, but who was a tremendous performer. He was an artist—today he would have been a film star.

---

market, many Cuban cigar makers relocated their factories to Florida and began recruiting Cuban factory laborers to work in them. By 1885, about three thousand Cubans were working in some one hundred cigar factories in Key West. Although they spent much of the year in the United States, these workers still considered themselves Cuban citizens. They frequently visited friends and relatives back in Cuba, traveling on a ferry that sailed between Key West and Havana three times a week.

The cigar manufacturers benefited from this ready supply of labor, but there was a problem. As an island, Key West was relatively isolated from the rest of the United States, making it a difficult place to do business as the cigar industry grew. In response, one factory owner, Vincente Martínez Ybor, decided to move his business to northern Florida in 1886. On forty acres of swampland north of the city of Tampa, Ybor built a large factory, along with cottages to serve as living quarters for his workers. Other cigar-factory owners soon followed Ybor's lead. The concentration of factories near Tampa, known both as "Ybor City" and "Cigar City," quickly supplanted Key West as the center of the cigar industry.

Moving their operations north solved one problem for the cigar manufacturers, but another, older problem remained. Cigar workers in Cuba often belonged to unions, which fought to keep their working conditions decent and their pay fair. When the cigar workers moved to the United States, they formed unions there as well, much to their employers' annoyance. The workers often went on strike when they believed factory owners were taking advantage of them.

The strikes did more than improve the laborers' working conditions: They helped unite the workers. They felt bonded to one another not only as Cubans, but also as members of the working class who faced the common problem of exploitation by their employers. This was an environment ideal for launching a revolution. All that was needed was a dynamic leader.

Planning the Revolution

As cigar workers were still flooding into Key West in 1881, a man who would change the course of Cuban history arrived in New York City: José Martí, a writer who had been deported because of his devotion to the cause of Cuban independence.

Although living more than one thousand miles from Cuba, Martí devoted himself to making his homeland free. He wrote essays advocating Cuban independence and collected funds to support the cause. In 1892 he founded the Partido Revolucionario Cubano (PRC), or the Cuban Revolutionary Party. He worked to bring all the Cubans in the United States into the party, which sought to spark another revolution in Cuba.

Uniting the Cuban immigrants proved to be a difficult task because of their divergent interests. The political exiles and *criollos* in the United States were fairly wealthy and upper class. They wanted Spain out of Cuba, but they did not want to see their wealth or positions threatened by a popular revolution. The cigar workers, on the other hand, were poor; many were also of African ancestry. They wanted to be free not only of Spanish control, but also of the racism and discrimination that kept black Cubans impoverished.

Through eloquent speeches, Martí worked to bridge the gap between these two groups. He spoke of a democratic Cuba, one that would provide justice for all, not just the rich and powerful. He soothed the misgivings of the *criollos* by envisioning a revolution that would bring more social equality without plunging the country into social chaos.

José Martí, founder of the Cuban Revolutionary Party, spoke of a democratic Cuba.

BETWEEN TWO WORLDS 19

Martí's message succeeded in winning the support of most Cuban expatriates. Martí also persuaded two rebel heroes of the Ten Years' War—Antonio Maceo and Máximo Gómez—to join the PRC. They organized groups of revolutionaries in Cuba while Martí planned an invasion of the island.

Martí on Cuban Independence

Cuban independence leader José Martí is considered one of the greatest political writers of his day. The following passage is from his essay "The Spanish Republic and the Cuban Revolution," which was published in Madrid, Spain, in February 1873.

Cuba calls for the independence to which it is entitled by life itself, which it knows it has; by the energetic steadfastness of its sons; by the richness of its territory; by the natural independence of that territory; and, more than anything else, because this is the firm, unanimous will of the Cuban people.

Spain feels that it must hold on to Cuba and cannot do so except . . . by trampling on its rights, imposing its will and staining its honor. . . . If it would end its domination over Cuba, it would bring imperishable glory to Spain. For too long, Spain has been beset by indecision and fear; let Spain at last have the courage to be glorious.

War Breaks Out

After years of preparation, the rebels were ready. Thousands of Cubans in the United States—including Martí, Maceo, and Gómez—headed for Cuba. In April 1895, they arrived at its shores ready to incite yet another revolution.

At first, the Spanish dismissed the invasion, confident that the rebellion would be easy to crush. But the rebels were well organized and, as they had hoped, many other Cubans joined their cause. Even José Martí's death in battle on May 19 did little to dampen the rebels' resolve. It became clear that, even without its leader, the revolution would continue.

In a show of contempt for their colonial masters, the rebels burned the plantations of wealthy Spaniards. The Spanish response was harsh. They came down hard on the rebel army, brutally slaughtering thousands of its troops. To prevent more Cubans from joining their ranks, they also herded more than three hundred thousand people into internment camps. Hunger and disease took the lives of many thousands of the internees.

Soon the turmoil in Cuba involved the United States. News of these civilian deaths made many Americans sympathetic to the Cuban rebels. Moreover, Americans who owned Cuban land and businesses feared that their investments would be destroyed in the conflict. Others relied on exporting goods to Cuba, a business that the revolution had put on hold. These businesspeople pushed the U.S. government to become involved and bring the war to an end.

Responding to this pressure, President William McKinley sent the U.S. warship

Well-organized Cuban rebels fought the Spanish for independence.

Maine into Havana's harbor to protect American citizens and property in Cuba. McKinley's move became the impetus for bringing the United States into the war. On February 15, 1898, the *Maine* exploded, killing 260 crew members. The American government blamed Spanish saboteurs for the explosion, although its actual cause was unknown at the time. Newspapers owned by William Randolph Hearst and Joseph Pulitzer also denounced the Spanish, while rallying Americans to action with the cry, "Remember the *Maine*." On April 25, 1898, the U.S. government declared war on Spain and sent troops to Cuba to aid the rebels.

What came to be known in the United States as the Spanish-American War was brief. Fighting alongside Cubans, American troops besieged Santiago de Cuba, Cuba's second largest city. On July 17, Spanish troops in the garrison at Santiago de Cuba surrendered. The Spanish government, concluding that it could no longer hold on to its colony, agreed to the island's independence. Less than three months after the United States joined the fight, the war was over.

Cuba was free, but for many Cubans, independence existed in name only. As soon as the Spanish left the island, the United States established a military occupation in Cuba to protect American interests there. Expressing the outrage of many Cubans, revolutionary leader Máximo Gómez declared: "Ours is the Cuban flag, the one for which so many tears and blood have been shed . . . we must keep united in order to bring an end to this unjustified military occupation."[5]

The United States removed its troops in 1902. However, in the final agreement calling for their withdrawl, it added the Platt Amendment—a set of provisions named after Orville H. Platt, the New York senator who fought for their inclusion. The Platt Amendment gave the United States the "right to intervene for the preservation of Cuban independence, the maintenance of a government adequate for the protection of life, property, and individual liberty."[6] Essentially, its provisions allowed the U.S. government to legally interfere in Cuban affairs.

In 1898, the battleship USS Maine, *shown here entering the Havana harbor, exploded, triggering the Spanish-American War.*

22   THE CUBAN AMERICANS

American troops land on a Cuban beach during the Spanish-American War.

Many Cubans greatly resented the Platt Amendment. During their hard-fought war, they had finally shaken off Spanish control over their government and their lives. Now it appeared they had only replaced one oppressor with another. With the powerful United States exerting its influence, free Cuba still seemed far from free.

CHAPTER TWO

Escaping Castro

As the twentieth century began, Cubans won their war to free themselves from Spanish control. But their fight to build their new nation had just begun. The first obstacle they faced was dealing with the devastation the Spanish-American War had wreaked on their land. Much of the nation's farmland had been destroyed, leaving people both homeless and unable to feed themselves. Not only the poor suffered in the war's aftermath. Their businesses and their land destroyed, many better-off Cubans were forced into debt and had no choice but to sell their property for far less than it was worth. Thousands of Americans came to Cuba and bought small-and medium-sized farms at bargain prices.

While Americans were flooding into Cuba, many Cubans, particularly members of the upper class, were making frequent trips to the United States. For those Cubans who had managed to hang on to their wealth, the United States had much to offer. In America, there were good private schools for their children to attend and better medical care for their families than they could find in their native country. The United States was also a shopper's paradise, full of consumer goods unavailable at home. Those who could afford a ticket could easily take steamships or ferries for a day's shopping excursion. Travel was made even easier in the 1940s and 1950s, when regular air service connected Havana to many major American cities.

Many Cubans also made frequent trips to the United States on business. American businesses in Cuba often hired well-educated Cubans to fill managerial jobs and other professional positions. Ambitious Cubans came to see the United States as a place to make a future for themselves. Among them was businessman Robert de Castro, who emigrated in 1943. He later explained, "My father, who had visited the United States, . . . encouraged me to migrate and repeatedly told me, 'That's the land of opportunity—go over there and seek your fortune. If it doesn't work out, then you come back.'"[7]

The 26th of July Movement

Following independence in 1902, Cuba's government experienced a series of crises. Factions vied for power, and corruption, even at the highest levels, was common. In

The Spanish-American War left many Cubans homeless and without food.

this chaotic political atmosphere, former president Fulgencio Batista took over the goverment in 1952 through a bloodless coup. Declaring himself dictator, Batista quickly proved to be a ruthless leader, crushing his political opponents. He also proved to be just as corrupt as many of his predecessors, as he funneled government money to his circle of supporters, making them rich while the average Cuban became increasingly impoverished. Batista also received money from American mobsters, who paid him to let them operate large resorts in Havana. Too expensive for the average Cuban to patronize, these resorts catered mostly to wealthy Americans, who treated Havana like their personal playground. In addition to featuring shows by the most popular American entertainers, the resorts often included large casinos. Dominated by mobsters, the Havana gambling industry put tens of millions of dollars into the pockets of American organized crime. The resorts also attracted prostitutes and drug dealers, who found many customers among vacationing Americans. Havanans soon blamed the tourists for encouraging these illegal activities to flourish in their city. In fact, many Cubans came to resent the presence of these Americans almost as much as they despised Batista and his men. As the anger of poor and powerless Cubans grew, the island was again ripe for revolution.

On July 26, 1953, a group of about one hundred poorly armed men stormed the Moncada Army Post in Santiago de Cuba, led by Fidel Castro, a twenty-seven-year-old former law student. Castro hoped that the attack would inspire people throughout Cuba to rise up against Batista. Government troops, however, crushed Castro's revolt in only a few minutes. Some of his men were killed. Others were captured and tortured. Castro himself was sentenced to fifteen years in prison.

The attack on Moncada at first seemed like a disaster, but the abortive attack earned Castro the status of a folk hero among ordinary Cubans. Seeing that keeping him locked up only increased Castro's following, in 1955 Batista gave Castro amnesty and released him from jail. Many Cubans saw Castro as their best hope for getting rid of Batista. Most of Castro's supporters were poor Cubans, although he also

Fulgencio Batista seized the government in 1952 and ruled with an iron fist.

Castro (far left) is arrested after an unsuccessful attack on Moncada.

attracted many students and intellectuals eager for a change. Castro's cause became known as the 26th of July Movement after the date of his unsuccessful attack on Moncada.

In November 1955, Castro made a trip to south Florida to persuade Cubans living in the United States to join his movement. He recruited a large number of followers among working-class Cubans, especially in Key West and Ybor City. They organized 26th of July clubs to raise money for Castro's rebel army.

Castro's message resonated with the workers regardless of their political beliefs. Carlos García, who emigrated to the United States in 1946, described the excitement Castro inspired during his visit: "We held a big rally and Fidel [Castro] spoke. And all of us who were against Batista, of different beliefs, we were there helping Fidel, this young man with a hope to get rid of the dictator. That was the feeling in those years. And we all got these great hopes that Fidel will be what he [said he will] be."[8]

Killing the Opposition

In 1959, when Cuban-born writer Flor Fernandez Barrios was four, Fidel Castro's revolutionaries wrested control of the Cuban government from dictator Fulgencio Batista. In her autobiography, Blessed by Thunder: Memoir of a Cuban Girlhood, *she remembered how her family and neighbors celebrated on hearing the news: "Glasses of wine went up in the air, toasting the long anticipated freedom from Batista's rule." The following day, however, their joy turned to terror as they heard that Castro's firing squads were hunting down all supposed enemies of the revolution.*

I was playing with my set of plastic army soldiers next to [my father] when our next-door neighbor and friend, Nena, came rushing through the front door.

"Felicia! Innocent people are getting killed by the milicianos [state police]. . . . You should have seen how those poor men were lined up, blindfolded and then sprayed with bullets from the machine guns of those criminals. Oh, my God!" Nena broke down in sobs. "The white wall turned red with their blood. I couldn't believe what my eyes were seeing."

Afraid for our safety, my mother and father decided it was best for us all to go and stay at my mother's parents' farm until things settled down in town. Without wasting any time, she packed a small suitcase with clothes and we started out on the eight-mile walk. "It is not safe to travel by car with all these crazy shootings," she said firmly. She thought the Revolutionaries were targeting the "fugitives" driving to the airports to escape to the United States with their fortunes and families. . . .

About a mile from my grandparents' farm, as we approached an orange grove, I saw the bodies of two men, each hung from the long branch of a big ateje tree on the side of the road. . . .

"Don't look," . . . I heard my mother say, but I couldn't pull my gaze away from the men. . . . They are always there, hanging in the darkness of my nights. I can see their tongues, long and purple, and their eyes, wide open to the sky.

Castro found less support from wealthier Cuban expatriates, though many were also disgusted by Batista and his regime. Castro promised to make sweeping social and economic reforms, aimed at spreading the nation's wealth more evenly among its citizens. The wealthiest Cubans were not eager to see these reforms enacted because if they were, the rich would likely lose both their wealth and their privileged position in Cuban society.

Castro and his supporters retreated into the Sierra Maestra, a mountain range in the southeastern part of the island, and gradually more and more Cubans joined them there. Despite Batista's efforts to put down

Castro's rebellion, the movement became stronger. At the same time, Batista lost the backing of the U.S. government. On March 14, 1958, the United States imposed an arms embargo on Cuba, which kept Batista from buying weapons from the United States.

With little means of defending his regime from Castro's 26th of July Movement, Batista saw that his days as Cuba's dictator were over. He and a small circle of friends fled the island on January 1, 1959. Learning that the hated dictator was gone, many Cubans rushed into the street to celebrate. Edmundo Alvarez Jr., then nine, later recalled, "[My family] got an early-morning call from one of my uncles saying that Batista had left the country. We heard noises outside, and we looked out the window—we saw all these red-and-black flags. . . . It was a party-type situation."[9]

The Cuban Revolution

With Batista gone, nothing stood in Castro's way. He marched to the Cuban capital of Havana, arriving there in triumph on January 8. In his memoirs, Cuban novelist and poet Pablo Medina described the scene:

> The whole city turned out to greet them. Women and children crowded round to kiss, to touch, to embrace them. Seeing a rebel on the street was enough to make the heart jump, for they were viewed with an awe bordering on the reverence reserved for saints. . . . Around their necks hung rosaries, religious medals, . . . and other mementos given to them by thankful citizens on their march to Havana.[10]

As Castro took control over the government, most Cubans—in Cuba and in the United States—rejoiced. He promised to institute a government that respected the human rights that Batista had long trampled upon.

Before long, however, it became clear that Cuba's new leader would not respect the rights of all Cubans. Castro began holding public trials, during which Batista's supporters were accused of being enemies of the revolution. Many were sentenced to die because of their opposition. Most Cubans, however, felt that these executions were just punishments for those who had supported the tyranny of Batista.

Many Cubans also believed that their lives would be better under Castro. People from the lower classes were especially encouraged by Castro's initial policies. He encouraged workers to go on strike for higher wages and often mediated with business owners on their behalf, ensuring that the strikes would be resolved in the workers' favor. He sharply reduced the amount of rent that landlords could charge, making housing much more affordable for poorer Cubans. Castro also aided the poor by offering them increased access to health care, education, and unemployment relief.

Castro's most sweeping reforms, however, focused on the use of land. Except for some sugar plantations and farms, he restricted the amount of land one person could own to one thousand acres. If someone owned more than one thousand acres, the excess land became the property of the goverment. (Castro offered compensation for this land, but the amount he paid was generally far lower than it was worth.) He also confiscated land and businesses owned by American companies, an action that greatly angered the U.S. government.

Soon, however, much of the early support for Castro began to fade as he instituted repressive policies to protect his power. He censored newspapers to prevent journalists from criticizing him. He ordered that schools teach children never to question his rule. He harassed the Catholic clergy and other religious leaders. One such incident was recalled by Ramon Fernandez, who came to the United States as a child in 1961: "One day there was a big hassle in the Catholic school. The guys came in with guns and started threatening nuns. Things like that. A couple of priests got beaten up. They were trying to stop all kinds of religion."[11] Thousands of Cubans found the atmosphere of fear and suspicion unbearable.

Under Castro's rule, land ownership was limited to one thousand acres; any excess went to the government.

Musicians and Athletes

During the early twentieth century, Cuban Americans were best known for their achievements in two fields—music and sports. Beginning in the 1920s, Cuban dances, such as the rumba, conga, mambo, bolero, and the cha-cha-cha, became crazes across the United States. Ernesto Lecuona, José Cubelo, Xavier Cugat, Desi Arnaz, and other musicians became important figures in the American jazz and big band scene.

In the world of athletics, Cuban Americans Kid Chocolate and Kid Gavilán were among the most famous boxers of the 1950s because of their regular appearances on the television program *Friday Night Fight*. During this era, Cubans' enthusiasm for baseball also came to the attention of American baseball leagues. Recognizing the island as a hotbed for talent, they recruited many star players from Cuba, including Cookie Rojas, Bert Campaneris, Pedro Ramos, and Sandy Amorós.

They felt they had no choice but to leave their country and find a new home.

Deciding to Leave

Although all Cubans who fled the country were discontented living under Castro, their specific reasons for leaving Cuba varied. The earliest immigrants were most concerned with saving their own lives. They were largely known as supporters of Batista and therefore they believed they would soon be facing Castro's firing squads. Among the first to leave were also wealthy Cubans whose lands and businesses were taken over by Castro's government. Prior to the revolution, some had invested money in banks in the United States and other countries. Left with nothing in Cuba, they moved abroad so they could continue to live well off their foreign investments.

For others, fear that Castro considered them an enemy made it impossible to stay in Cuba. Early in his regime, Castro declared that "for the revolution everything is acceptable and against it nothing."[12] For scholars, writers, and other intellectuals, this statement was a warning. If Castro loyalists heard them voicing any criticism of his firing squads and other repressive measures, their words would be reported to the authorities, who responded with harsh punishments. A person who expressed even mild discontentment with the government might face many years in prison, or worse. For intellectuals who refused to stay quiet, the only means of saving themselves was fleeing the country. Among them was Irma de Leon, who had been a judge under Batista's rule. She later recalled:

> The Revolution brought an abrupt change to my life. Everything that I had been taught and stood for changed. Castro appeared on television and reported, "Last night we passed a law and

everybody who doesn't agree with it will be put into prison." I knew then I would have to leave or they would kill me. In May 1962 I made a decision to leave Cuba.[13]

Many other Cubans became disillusioned with Castro as he struggled to restructure the Cuban economy. With the United States no longer willing to trade with Cuba, Castro tried to find other markets for Cuban exports such as sugar, but his efforts were mostly unsuccessful. He also attempted to bolster the economy by increasing Cuba's food production and developing new industries. These economic policies, however, mostly foundered, in large measure because the new Cuban government was too inexperienced to implement them effectively. Soon, the country was faced with severe shortages of food and other necessities. Average Cubans had to survive on modest food rations provided by the government. The daily stress of coping with such scarcities helped drive many people from Cuba. Among them was Roberto Ortiz, who fled the country in 1962. He later remembered:

> Things started to get tough. . . . You could not get food. . . . When you go and see a relative and they don't have food to put on the table, this is bad! When you walk in there, and they are waiting for you to leave, to eat. And when you got to do the same thing at home—I couldn't live with it, and decided to leave from a combination of all these things.[14]

Another factor in many immigrants' decision to leave Cuba was Castro's failure to restore democracy to the island. Initally, some Cubans had supported Castro because they hoped he would hold free elections and abide by the old Cuban constitution—which Batista had disavowed when he rose to power. But it soon became clear that all real power in the new government would be held by Castro alone. Some Cubans were greatly embittered by Castro's failure to make democratic reforms. They were so desperate to live in a democracy that they were willing to abandon their native country. Speaking of these immigrants, Rafael Peñalver, a Cuban American attorney, explained:

> These were people who had it all in Cuba. They were living comfortable lives, they were professionals, they were well-adjusted, and they gave it all up because they wanted their children to live in an environment of freedom . . . where their children could grow and develop their full potential—something they couldn't do in Cuba.[15]

Finding a New Country

Regardless of their reasons, after reaching the difficult decision to leave Cuba, immigrants had to make another important choice—where to go. Some Cubans resettled in Mexico, Spain, Venezeula, and other Spanish-speaking countries. In addition to a common language, many aspects of these countries' cultures, such as their religious customs, were familiar, making the adjustment to life there relatively easy. Also, for some of these emigrants, memories of American interference in Cuban affairs since the nineteenth century left them so embittered that they had no interest in living in the United States.

For Cubans without intense anti-American feelings, however, the United States had much to offer. First, its proximity to Cuba; with Miami only ninety miles away, emigrants needed to take only a forty-five-minute plane trip to reach the U.S. mainland. The United States was also appealing to Cubans who had spent time there on vacations or business trips. Even if they were not fluent in English, they were at least familiar with American customs. In addition, most Cubans had some ties to the United States, thanks to the many Cubans who already were living there. In 1959, when Castro came into power, about thirty thousand Cubans lived in Miami, Florida, alone. Emigrants, therefore, generally had a relative, a friend, or at least a friend of a friend already living in the United States on whom they could call for help and support.

Due to poor living conditions, many people fled Cuba and resettled in Mexico and the United States.

The Trip North

Initially, it was relatively easy for Cubans to leave. They did not even have to declare that they were emigrating to the United States for good. All they had to do was claim they were traveling as tourists and apply for an exit permit from the Cuban Interior Ministry. Furthermore, because Castro was eager to rid Cuba of all who might oppose his policies, most emigrants obtained the permits with little difficulty, regardless of what officials thought their intentions might be.

A few would-be emigrants ran into trouble, however. The ministry sometimes refused to issue them to young, healthy men eligible to be drafted into Castro's army. People who were suspected of being enemies of the revolution were also not given permits. Castro wanted to make an example out of these people by punishing them with long prison sentences. Fearing persecution, some sought refuge in foreign embassies, where they stayed—sometimes for years—while embassies' staffs tried to arrange their escape.

By the end of 1961, the Cuban government became alarmed that many of the country's best educated and most successful citizens were fleeing to the United States. To stem the tide of this "brain drain," it made the emigration process more difficult. Applicants for exit permits had to fill out long forms and submit to lengthy interrogations by Cuban officials. They were also required to pay for their plane tickets in U.S. dollars, which meant emigrants often had to wait for friends and relatives in the United States to send them the money

The Cuban government became worried when successful citizens, like the ones shown, began fleeing the country.

Desi Arnaz

A band leader and television star, Desi Arnaz was the most famous Cuban American of the early twentieth century. He was born Desiderio Alberto Arnaz y De Acha into an upper-class family in Santiago, Cuba, on March 2, 1917. His father was the city's mayor, and his mother was the heiress to the Bacardi Rum fortune.

In 1933 the family was forced to leave Cuba because of its association with President Gerardo Machado, who was overthrown in a political coup. After settling in Miami, the once-prosperous Arnazes were penniless, dashing the family's dream that Desi would become a lawyer. Instead, he worked odd jobs, including singing and playing guitar in a hotel band. He was soon discovered by Xavier Cugat, then known as the king of Latin music. Arnaz briefly sang with Cugat's orchestra before establishing his own band in 1937.

After making his Broadway debut in the musical *Too Many Girls,* Arnaz headed to Los Angeles to appear in the movie adaptation. On the set, he met actress Lucille Ball, whom he married in 1940. Hoping to develop a television show in which they both could star, Arnaz and Ball founded Desilu, a production company, in 1950.

Initially, they had trouble finding a network willing to take their show, largely because television executives as-

Desi Arnaz became a popular band leader and television star in the United States.

sumed that Arnaz's strong Cuban accent would turn off viewers. However, when the show, titled *I Love Lucy,* premiered in 1951, it was an immediate hit. Playing a bandleader, Arnaz became the most popular Hispanic American performer in the United States. Arnaz largely fell out of the public eye after his divorce from Ball in 1960. Since his death in 1986, he has been remembered as a beloved entertainer and a talented television pioneer.

they needed. Even after the money arrived, they sometimes faced a long wait to book a seat as the government reduced the number of flights leaving Cuba.

People who decided to emigrate to the United States knew that everything they left behind—houses, cars, and personal possessions—would be confiscated by the Cuban government. In fact, as soon as a family began planning to leave the country, government officials started eyeing their assets, as Roberto Ortiz, who emigrated in 1962, recalled:

> The moment you submit the papers, you're not supposed to get anything out of the house. On every block they had a watching committee, watching everything you do. These people will watch you twenty-four hours a day, all your movements. When you leave, everything that you left inside—a watching committee would come and make an inventory and seal the house. They'd put paper in there with glue on the door and lock them up. And that was the end of it. You lose everything. Whatever was inside, it's the government property.[16]

By law, travelers could bring with them only five U.S. dollars and thirty pounds of luggage. The restrictions meant that they could pack only their most treasured possessions. Even these were often taken from them at the airport by Cuban police, who rifled through the travelers' luggage searching for jewelry and other valuables. Sometimes, police even forced emigrants to disrobe and subjected them to humiliating strip searches.

As one emigrant remembered: "At the airport, the *milicianos* [state police] made us disrobe and they checked all our personal belongings. Everybody . . . even babies in diapers . . . even old people. They were so arrogant, those *milicianos*. But we didn't say anything because if we did, they wouldn't let us leave."[17]

The stress that emigrants endured did not let up until their airplanes left Cuban airspace. Police frequently took passengers off a plane before takeoff for further interrogation. To harass the already frightened travelers, Cuban authorities also sometimes called back an airplane in midflight. Only when a plane had passed into American airspace were emigrants confident that they would finally arrive in the United States. One woman described the intense sadness passengers felt, as from the plane's windows they watched their beloved Cuba fade into the distance: "On the plane everybody was quiet. . . . We were all heartbroken. Many people were crying; others just sat there staring off into space. We were leaving our country for who knows how long. We were leaving everything behind."[18] But as they neared the United States, the mood of the emigrants shifted to one of jubilation: "Halfway into the flight the pilot announced that we were in U.S. territory. . . . Everybody started clapping and cheering. Some men started cursing Fidel Castro . . . and his mother."[19] However difficult it was to get there, touching down in the United States was really only the beginning of a hard journey for these Cuban emigrants. Once on American soil, they faced the long and difficult task of building a new life in a new land.

CHAPTER THREE

The Golden Exiles

The Cubans who came to the United States in the wake of Castro's rise to power were mostly well educated, and many were from Cuba's upper classes. At home, these people had held well-paying jobs, working in such professional fields as medicine, law, and education. Many were well-off and accustomed to living in comfortable homes, where they were waited on by servants. However, this good life of the Golden Exiles—as they became known in the United States—was lost the moment they left Cuba. Forced to leave behind almost all their money and possessions, they began their life in the United States with nothing.

Settling In

For most of the exiles, the first stop in the United States was the Miami area, and the majority chose to settle close by. They liked the climate in south Florida, which reminded them of Cuba's. Also, there had been a small contingent of Cubans living in Miami already, so many of the immigrants had a relative—or at least an acquaintance—who could help them get back on their feet. Some, too, wanted to remain close to Cuba so they could quickly return if Castro were overthrown.

Most of the immigrants moved to southwest Miami, where rents were low. Even so, few families could afford their own house.

Several families often pooled their resources and together moved into a small apartment. Many later opened their cramped quarters to old friends and family members who had just arrived in Miami with nowhere else to stay.

As difficult as these living conditions were, at least anyone in need knew there were friends nearby who would be willing to lend a hand. Neighbors gave each other rides to work and shops and shared information about job openings. Cuban American author Gustavo Pérez Firmat wrote in his memoirs that, as a child, the enforced togetherness made life in America "an adventure. . . . It was exciting sleeping three or four to a room, having people come and go all the time, packing everyone into the Rambler and going to the Tropicaire drive-in on a steamy summer night."[20] For children and adults alike, just having other Cubans around them helped relieve the emotional trauma of being uprooted from their home. Those homesick for Cuba could always find someone to talk to about their memories of the past and their hope for the future.

Although most assumed they would soon be returning home, the exiles had to seek out at least temporary work to survive. No matter how well educated they were, most had to settle for low-paying, low-prestige jobs. Some could not speak English well enough

Cuban Americans living in Miami find comfort among friends and relatives.

to find any other work. Others, such as doctors or lawyers, could not legally practice their profession until they obtained licenses in the United States. In the meantime, they parked cars, washed dishes, drove taxis, waited tables—any work they could find to put food on their families' tables.

Relief for the Needy

Relief organizations, many of which were operated by the Catholic Church, pitched in to help struggling exile families. For instance, Centro Hispano Católico in downtown Miami offered Cubans help in finding jobs and housing and conducted English classes and other educational programs. For immigrants in dire need, it provided small loans, food, and toiletries.

These relief organizations were soon overwhelmed by the growing demands for their services. Between 1959 and 1962, more than 250,000 Cubans flew from Havana to Miami. To help deal with this flood of immigrants, most of whom chose to settle in southern Florida, a group of Miami civic leaders calling themselves the Cuban Refugee Committee made an appeal for help to President Dwight D. Eisenhower in October 1960. The Eisenhower administration responded by establishing the Cuban Refugee Emergency Center. The center coordinated the various relief organizations' activities.

Initially, however, the federal government itself provided little money for relief. It instead focused its efforts on resettling the Cubans in cities throughout the United States to relieve the saturation that the mass immigration had placed on Miami's schools and social welfare programs. Government workers, with stories of better housing and good jobs available in other areas, tried to convince the immigrants to leave Florida. Wanting to remain among friends and relatives, most of the immigrants, however, had no interest in settling elsewhere.

After assuming office in 1961, President John F. Kennedy expanded the federal services available for Cubans by establishing the Cuban Refugee Program. It offered exile families monthly one-hundred-dollar relief checks, free health care, and loans for

---

Municipios

To help one another adjust to life in the United States, the Cuban exiles established *municipios*. These organizations offered English classes, job information, and emergency aid to families in need. They also provided a way for people to hold on to their Cuban identity. In addition to hosting celebrations of traditional holidays, the *municipios* brought together people who had been neighbors on the island. Each organization was named after one of the 126 *municipios,* or townships, then in Cuba. By joining the *municipio* named after the town where they used to live, immigrants could easily maintain ties with old colleagues and friends.

Over time, as Cuban immigrants grew familiar with their new country, the *municipios* became more concerned with political issues. The many *municipios* now in operation in Miami are largely political organizations devoted to promoting democracy in Cuba.

college. The modest aid, however, was hardly adequate for many immigrants. Rodolfo de León, who arrived in the United States in 1962 at age eleven, recalled how his family struggled to survive:

> The second or third week we were here we started receiving help from the government. We collected some food, and we got $100 a month. . . . After a month or something like that we found this other place, which was $72. We were renting the apartment for $72, and so we had $28 for the month. That meant a dollar a day. We lived on that for I think a year and a half.[21]

The government also gave funds to the Miami public school system so that it could accommodate thousands of new Cuban students. Still, the schools struggled to accommodate the flood of immigrant children. In addition to increasing class sizes, teaching the children posed a challenge to the city's teachers, most of whom did not speak Spanish. Mirta R. Vega, a Cuban immigrant who briefly worked as a teacher's aide, described the crisis.

> My students were all Cuban refugee children and they were very frightened. . . . Each day two or three or four new refugee children arrived at the school. . . . New classes had to be created all the time. Some of the teachers just couldn't handle it. One day, two American teachers came up to me and said, "Don't take it personally, but we've decided to take early retirement. The changes here are just too much for us."[22]

Operation Pedro Pan

In early 1961 the U.S. government initiated an effort to help Cuban exiles. It provided aid to bring Cuban children to the United States under the Unaccompanied Cuban Children's Program, unofficially known as Operation Pedro Pan. The operation was the brainchild of James Baker, the headmaster of a private school in Havana, and Bryan Walsh, a priest who served as director of Miami's Catholic Welfare Bureau. The program's initial goal was to bring two hundred Cuban children to the United States. The children's lives were in danger because their parents were working to overthrow Castro and were therefore regarded as enemies of the state.

Soon, with the U.S. government's help, Walsh, Baker, and a group of sympathetic Cubans expanded Operation Pedro Pan to get thousands more young people onto U.S.-bound flights, even though their parents were not allowed to leave Cuba. Many parents were eager to send their children off alone because they did not want them eventually drafted into the Cuban army. Some also were frightened by rumors that Castro planned to send their children away to be educated in the Soviet Union. Nearly all the parents assumed their separation from their children would be brief. They expected Castro's regime to fall in a matter of months, after which they could send for their children to come home.

A Miami reporter gave the program its nickname, invoking the fictional character Peter Pan, a boy who could fly and never wanted to grow up. But Elly Chovel, one of the Cubans who came to the United States on the flights, observed that the name was hardly appropriate. In 1999, she recalled,

"[Peter] Pan flew off and didn't want to grow up. We flew away and had to grow up in a hurry."[23] Although older children often saw the trip as an adventure, they often found themselves responsible for comforting and caring for their younger siblings. The youngest of the Pedro Pan children were only three or four. When they arrived in Miami, they were often inconsolable, frightened and confused about where they were and why their parents had sent them away.

Before the program was suspended in 1962, more than fourteen thousand Cuban children came to the United States as part of Operation Pedro Pan. Some children were soon reunited with their parents, once they, too, found a way to leave Cuba. But many other children were not so lucky. They were sent to live in foster homes and orphanages, often for many years. A few never saw their parents again after leaving Havana.

Operation Pedro Pan was responsible for bringing more than fourteen thousand Cuban children to the United States.

THE GOLDEN EXILES 41

Miamians versus Cubans

The plight of the Pedro Pan children was reported in newspapers throughout the country. Initially, Americans were highly supportive of Cuban immigrants—both children and adults. They were impressed by the substantial sacrifices the immigrants chose to make in order to live in a free society. But every day, as hundreds more Cubans arrived, some people, particularly those in the Miami

---

Lessons of Pedro Pan

In preparing her book Operation Pedro Pan: The Untold Exodus of 14,048 Cuban Children, *writer Yvonne M. Conde sent questionnaires to eight hundred Cuban Americans who came to the United States as children on the Pedro Pan flights of the early 1960s. Several shared with Conde what they believed their experiences had taught them as adults.*

Susan Garrandes:
This separation made me very intolerant with people who think it is the end of the world because they couldn't buy themselves a lipstick. Come on, wake up, smell the coffee. You've got food on the table and a roof over your head? Be happy. You become very intolerant of people who are always crying and whining about things that are not really important. You also put a lot of weight on family and unity and that kind of stuff. You don't want to be without it.

Roberto Zaldivar:
As another child refugee once told me, "We have been marked for life," and it is true. Our experience has made us different, made us mature ahead of time. Gave us responsibilities that we did not need to have at such an early age, yet made us value many things that other people don't value at all. I have seen people my age blaming their parents for all this. And it is not the fault of our parents, but the fault of a government on our land who made us and them do what we did—decide to leave our homeland.

Ilena Fuentes:
When my daughter was eleven, I sent her to Tampa for a week's vacation at my cousin's. . . . When she boarded the plane, . . . I was on the other side of the glass and all the suffering of [my separation from my parents], the anguish by default, that I felt in that moment was so horrible that I spent the afternoon crying. . . . In that moment I corroborated how traumatic this separation had been for me. . . . And I always say that having gone through the experience I would never separate from my daughter. Never.

Antonia Martínez:
When you are smaller you don't realize what adults are going through. . . . I keep thinking back to the different instances, the decisions that [my parents] had to make and the choices. They were very difficult choices I don't know if I would have been able to do it the same way or not. I guess if you are faced with that choice at the time, that is the choice that you had to make.

Spanish street signs reflect the significant presence of Cuban Americans in the Miami, Florida, area.

area, became less welcoming to the flood of new immigrants.

At the time, Miami was suffering an economic recession. Jobs were hard to find, so native Miamians were angry that they now had to compete with Cuban immigrants for work. Also, many Cubans were so desperate for work that they would accept extremely low wages, which had the effect of driving down workers' pay throughout the city. Needy native Miamians were further annoyed that Cubans had access to more federal financial aid than they did. In a letter to the editor of a local newspaper, one woman bitterly complained about what she saw as an overly generous national policy toward the immigrants: "I sincerely think that our president is letting down his people again, sacrificing our welfare and security further for Cubans who will not appreciate it and . . . will stab us in the back every chance they get."[24]

Cuban culture also alarmed some Miamians. In particular, whites in Miami had little experience dealing with people from other races or ethnic backgrounds. To some Miamians, Cubans, with their unfamiliar customs and language, were unwelcome foreigners. Cuban American banker Luis Botifoll described the tensions that simmered between native Miamians and the Cuban newcomers in the early 1960s: "Some people resented our presence here because we speak a different language, we were talking too loud, we didn't have enough money and, when we rented an apartment, a two-room apartment, maybe seven or eight relatives would move in. So, they had signs saying, 'No Cubans, no pets, and no children.'"[25]

THE GOLDEN EXILES

People participating in an anti-Castro protest.

Fighting Castro

Soon, however, a different view of the Cuban immigrants emerged. Many articles in local and national newspapers and magazines celebrated their industriousness and praised their willingness to suffer to live in a free society.

The U.S. government encouraged publications to promote this view of the Golden Exiles. By supporting the Cuban immigrants, it hoped to rally public support for its opposition to Castro. In addition to his violation of Cubans' civil rights, Castro angered the U.S. government by making anti-American speeches and by refusing to compensate American businesses for their land and assets in Cuba, which his government seized. Perhaps even more alarming for government policy makers, Castro announced that Cuba was now a communist nation. He also had started accepting aid from the greatest communist superpower, the Soviet Union, seemingly giving America's greatest adversary a foothold in the Western Hemisphere.

While praising the Cuban immigrants as freedom loving, the United States also encouraged exiles who hoped to incite a counterrevolution in Cuba. As a result, in the Cuban community of Miami, more than fifty political organizations were created. At meetings, members of these organizations had spirited discussions about the future of Cuba. Although they did not always agree on what type of government they wanted for their native land, they all shared the dream of one day reclaiming Cuba from Castro.

Brigade 2506

Some immigrants tried to turn their dream into reality. Backed by the CIA, in February 1961, some fifteen hundred men began training for an invasion of Cuba. The group called themselves Brigade 2506. The name came from the number assigned to recruit Carlos "Carlay" Rodriguez Santana, who had been killed early on during a training accident.

The brigade was supposed to train in secret so that their invasion would take Castro's army by surprise. But in Miami, people in the Cuban community began noticing that certain men had mysteriously vanished and that their families were receiving financial support from the U.S. government. From this evidence, rumors spread that the United States was at last organizing the hoped-for overthrow of Castro.

The *Miami Herald* investigated the rumors and discovered the government's plans. At first, the newspaper opted not to print the story, for fear of undermining the invasion. The newspaper changed its mind, however, after other papers and magazines started reporting on the "secret" operation. A prominent article in the *New York Times* even published a map of the training camp

---

The Brigade 2506 Association

The survivors of Brigade 2506 are still considered heroes in the Cuban American community. The Bay of Pigs Museum and Library in Little Havana displays maps, uniforms, and arms of the brigade, as well as photographs of those killed during the invasion and afterward in Cuban prisons. Brigade members are also honored at an annual ceremony held on April 17, the date the invasion began. According to the Brigade 2506 Association's website, association president Juan E. Pérez-Franco said the following words at the 1998 festivities:

As we have been doing yearly, today, the 38th anniversary of the Invasion of the Bay of Pigs, the members of Brigade 2506 offer well deserved homage, admiration and respect to our fallen brothers and to all of those who have given their lives striving to free our country....

We send a message of support and solidarity to the Cuban people; to those farmers who were cheated by the Agrarian Reform; to those workers who are being used as slaves by the foreign firms who exploit them; to the youth that does not have the opportunity of developing and the members of the armed forces who do not belong to the governing elite and suffer the same as the rest of the Cuban population.

Enough of bloodshed, jails and suffering. Let's unite our efforts, we here and they over there, and with the help of God let's once and for all end the Castro-Communist tyranny.

The 2506 Brigade is and will always be, faithful to the war cry that started in the bloody sands of [the Bay of Pigs], ... which has always been and will always be our guide: We shall never forsake our country.

the brigade had established in Guatemala. Brigade member Manolo Llerena described the tension the news coverage spread among the troops:

> It was difficult to keep morale up and there were many security leaks. Some of us spent eighteen months in camp without much to do except train.... Every time the news leaked, the CIA would postpone the plans.... Every delay brought new anxieties and more dissensions. When we finally left Guatemala, the camp was about to explode.[26]

The Bay of Pigs Invasion

Despite the undesired publicity, the CIA went forward with the mission beginning on April 17, 1961. The invasion plan called for Brigade 2506 to rush ashore at the Bay of Pigs. The CIA assumed that, as soon as the Cuban people learned of the troops' presence, they would join the fight.

Castro, however, was ready for the invaders. Tipped off by news accounts, he had organized twenty thousand troops ready to battle the brigade. To prevent any problems with local opposition, Castro also rounded up and placed in detention camps one hundred thousand Cubans who had expressed

Members of Castro's militia during the Bay of Pigs invasion.

dissatisfaction with his rule. One of those taken to camps was student Manuel Salvat, who later described the ordeal: "April 17th, for us, was a great frustration. We woke up to the news that the invasion had arrived and we, simply, were not ready. The regime was apprehending anyone who looked a bit suspicious; . . . I [got] caught during a routine search . . . [and was detained] for 18 days."[27] With most possible sympathizers detained, only about fifty Cubans came out to fight with the brigade. Also hobbling the invasion, President John F. Kennedy, hoping to minimize American involvement in the mission, at the last minute reduced the amount of air support provided by the United States.

When Cubans in America heard of the Bay of Pigs invasion, they gathered in parks, cafes, and churches, anxiously sharing whatever news they had with one another. After two days, they learned that the mission had turned into a disaster. Castro's troops had quickly surrounded the brigade and captured the soldiers, one by one.

Suffering Defeat

The Bay of Pigs was a humiliation to the United States and a public relations triumph for Castro. He had outsmarted one of the world's superpowers, and in the process elevated his reputation throughout the world. Before the Bay of Pigs, he had been seen as an unpredictable revolutionary with a shaky hold on an unstable government. Afterward, he seemed to be a savvy leader able to take on the powerful United States and win.

The Cuban exiles were appalled. They had prayed the invasion would remove Castro from power once and for all. Instead, Castro not only still ruled Cuba, but he also had more power than ever. To the rest of the world, he seemed to be a savvy leader able to take on the powerful United States and win. Many in the immigrant community blamed the U.S. government for the botched military operation. Echoing the sentiments of many, Cuban immigrant José Basulto maintained in an interview with scholar Miguel Gonzalez-Pando that the "defeat of the invasion was due to a lack of U.S. support, when it failed to honor the promises to provide air support and to aid the underground. Our fundamental error was placing Cuba's destiny on the hands of the United States."[28]

Rescuing the Brigade

The rage of Cuban immigrants only grew as negotiations stalled for the release of the Brigade 2506 members who had survived the fighting. The immigrants were horrified when they learned in March 1962 that the captured soldiers had each been sentenced to thirty years in a Cuban prison. Castro agreed to ransom the prisoners, but kept upping his price, eventually asking for a total of $62 million. The U.S. government, not wanting to be seen as bowing to Castro's will, refused to pay the ransom. The Cuban immigrant community, therefore, went about raising the sum through private donations.

Among the organizations established to collect the ransom was the Cuban Families Committee for the Release of Cuban Prisoners of War. Comprising Cuban immigrants, it sold "Freedom Medallions," each featuring the number of a brigade member as part of its fundraising campaign. In addition, it arranged for stories about the Cuban

Cuban soldiers line up captured members of Brigade 2506.

prisoners to appear in such magazines as *Life* and *Reader's Digest*. Through the committee's efforts, Ed Sullivan, the host of a top-rated television variety show, was also persuaded to make an on-air appeal for contributions to the cause. According to banker Claudio Sanchez, the campaign helped unite the Cubans of Miami:

> There were many months when we feared for the well-being of our captured men. There was, I think, a feeling of unity among the Cubans, and also between the Cubans and the rest of the community. We came together like we never had before.... It was then that I think we began to see each other as members of a group, a social group.[29]

Castro finally agreed to accept a ransom of $53 million worth of goods that were in short supply in Cuba. The shipment included baby food, powdered milk, medicines, and pesticides, much of which was donated by American corporations. On December 23, 1961, the prisoners were at last returned to the United States and reunited with their families. The next day, they were treated to a hero's welcome before a crowd of forty thousand—including President Kennedy and his wife Jacqueline—at Miami's Orange Bowl stadium. During the ceremony, Kennedy told the brigade members:

> Your small brigade is a tangible reaffirmation that the human desire for freedom and independence is essentially unconquerable. Your conduct and valor are proof that, although Castro and his fellow dictators may rule nations, they do not rule people; that they may imprison bodies, but they do not imprison spirits; that they may destroy the exercise of liberty, but they cannot eliminate the determination to be free.[30]

In the event's most moving moment, the soldiers gave the president one of the brigade's flags, prompting him to say, "I can assure you that this flag will be returned to this Brigade in a free Havana."[31] The off-the-cuff remark again stirred hope in many of the exiled Cubans. Although many exiles felt that the United States had failed them with the Bay of Pigs, they prayed that Kennedy might still find a way to oust the hated Castro.

The Cuban Missile Crisis

The idea of a second invasion soon faded, however, as Kennedy was caught up in what came to be known as the Cuban Missile Crisis. In October 1962, U.S. spy planes detected missile launching sites in Cuba that were capable of sending nuclear warheads to almost any location in the United States. The warheads were supplied to Cuba by the Soviet Union. President Kennedy ordered a blockade of Cuba to keep missiles from being shipped to the island and demanded that the Soviet Union remove the launching sites.

The thirteen-day standoff over the missiles brought the United States and the Soviet Union to the brink of nuclear war. While the entire world waited nervously to see how the crisis would play out, some Cuban exiles were excited by the dangerous developments. They hoped that the crisis would inspire the United States to bring down Castro once and for all.

In fact, the Cuban Missile Crisis had the opposite effect. In the end, the Soviet Union agreed to remove the missiles rather than risk nuclear war. As part of their agreement, Kennedy promised not to sponsor any further invasions of Cuba. Any hope of a quick return home still lingering in the Cuban exile community was finally extinguished.

Facing Facts

The missile crisis also had the effect of further squeezing off the flow of Cuban immigration to the United States. During the missile crisis, Castro put an end to the regular flights between Havana and Miami, making immigration to the United States far more difficult. Because of Castro's anger toward the United States, would-be immigrants found that even applying for an exit permit to America could make them targets of persecution by the Cuban government. The only safe way a Cuban could come to the United States was to travel first to another country, such as Spain and Mexico, and then immigrate to the United States from there. The process was time consuming, complicated, and expensive. As a result, for many Cuban exiles, being reunited with relatives still in Cuba became an impossible dream.

In the wake of the missile crisis, Cubans in the United States were dealt another blow as the CIA began to disband all covert operations designed to overthrow Castro. This move affected more than just the immigrants' morale. By the early 1960s, the CIA had had about twelve thousand Cuban immigrants on its payroll. Suddenly, these people found themselves unemployed. Furthermore, after years of encouraging various exile groups to launch small commando raids in Cuba, the U.S. government started discouraging such operations for fear they would spark another international crisis. Some Cuban exiles were even prosecuted by the U.S. Justice Department for using the training and arms originally provided to them by the CIA.

In the aftermath of the Cuban Missile Crisis, the Cubans in the United States had to face some difficult facts. They had placed their trust in the U.S. government to save Cuba from Castro, and, in their view at least, the government had let them down. Many had assumed their stay in the United States would be temporary. Now like it or not, they would have to build new lives in a land not their own.

CHAPTER FOUR

Blending Old and New

By 1963 the Cuban exiles had given up hope that the United States would lead the way in overthrowing Castro. And with few funds of their own, they could not themselves afford to assemble and arm an army large enough to bring Castro down. Although the exiles still dreamed that one day they would return home, most faced the reality that they could not count on going back to Cuba anytime soon.

With this realization, the Cubans in America began refocusing their energy on a new goal—proving their worth in their new home. To discredit the exiles, Castro had told the Cuban people that those who left the country were traitors. He called them "worms" and "the scum of the earth." Castro's taunts only made the exiles more eager to show the world what they could do. According to exile Luis Aguilar León, who became a professor at Georgetown University,

> Castro was calling us "worms" . . . [and saying that] we were of no value whatsoever. And there was a sort of silent code or effort to say, wherever I am—and I have heard this from many mechanics, professors, writers, and lawyers—wherever I am, I am going to demonstrate that I am a Cuban and that I am very good at what I do.[32]

In addition to proving their value as a group, the exiles also wanted to demonstrate the flaws in the communism Castro had embraced. One of the exiles' means of doing this was to prove that capitalism could lead to a better life. Toward this end, many Cubans resolved to work hard and become financially secure. By succeeding financially, they hoped not only to provide a better future for themselves and their families. They also wanted to demonstrate the superiority of capitalism, thereby challenging Castro's claims that communism would make Cuba a better place to live.

The Resettlement Program

With their newfound determination to succeed in the United States, some Cubans reevaluated their decision to live in Miami. Because of the flood of immigrants into the area, finding work or even renting an apartment in the city had become increasingly difficult. Even though in Miami they were among friends and family, some exiles came to the conclusion that they would have a better chance of prospering in a location where the competition for jobs and housing was not as fierce. They decided to settle elsewhere with the help of the U.S. government's Cuban Refugee Program (CRP).

With brochures and films touting the courage of the exiles, the CRP sought out civic and church groups across the nation to sponsor Cuban families. As sponsors, these groups were expected to help the Cubans get their financial footing and generally adjust to American life. The CRP also worked to

Capitalism flourishes in this Cuban American neighborhood.

overcome the objections the immigrants had to relocating. It tried to settle three or four families together in one area, so they also had at least a few other exiles to rely on for psychological and emotional support. In the CRP's early years, the program also promised to arrange for resettled Cubans to travel back to Miami in the event that Castro's regime came to an end, allowing them to return to Cuba.

For some exiles, however, the promise of employment was enough to motivate them to request resettlement through the CRP. A teaching job, for instance, enticed Sofia Rodriguez into moving to the Midwest:

> When we arrived in Miami, my husband and I went to the refugee center. We completed the applications and looked for work.... They called us after some time, and they said there was an opportunity in Bluffton, Indiana. There was a church that wanted to sponsor a Cuban family and a high school that needed a Spanish teacher. There was our opportunity, even though we didn't know where Bluffton, Indiana, was.[33]

Others were persuaded by the CRP's appeal to the exiles' patriotism. Program officials told exiles that if they spread out across the country, they could inform Americans everywhere about the evils of Castro and communism. When persuasion failed to convince many immigrants to resettle, the government applied not-so-subtle pressure. In 1964, President Lyndon B. Johnson announced that any unemployed Cubans in Miami would lose benefits administered by the CRP if they refused to settle elsewhere. John F. Thomas, the CRP's director, states that the policy was "designed to encourage the refugee who is caught in a vicious web of uncertainty, dependency, and propaganda to face the realities of life."[34]

Through the resettlement program and the exiles' own initiative, thousands of Cubans moved to more than twenty-five hundred areas throughout the United States. Most went to Union City, New Jersey; New York; Chicago; Boston; Washington, D.C.; and other urban centers. For some resettled exiles, especially children, being thrown into an environment dominated by Americans and their unfamiliar ways was difficult. In his memoir *Exiled Memories: A Cuban Childhood,* poet Pablo Medina recalled his bewilderment as a child when he first encountered the aggressive behavior of teachers and students at his new school in New York City:

> J.H.S. 167 was a typical New York school, a microcosm of the city where all races mingled and fought and, on occasion, learned.... On that first day I was witness to a scene that was to totally alter my image of what school was. On my way from one class to the next, I saw a teacher—who, I later learned, was the prefect of discipline—dragging a girl away by the arm. The girl, trying to tug herself free, was screaming. He slapped her across the face several times.... I ... stared, frozen by violence in a place previous experience had deluded me into thinking ought to be quiet and genteel and orderly.[35]

But others, such as Sofia Rodriguez's daughter Alicia, found Americans surprisingly friendly. She remembered her new neighbors

The *Quinceañera*

For many Cuban American women, their *quinceañera* ranks as one of the most important events of their lives. Often called a *quince,* the celebration is held on a girl's fifteenth birthday in many Hispanic cultures. It marks the moment she becomes a woman in the eyes of her community. After a girl's *quince,* her family often gives her more freedom to date and wear makeup, but she is also expected to take on additional responsibilities around the house.

A *quince* begins in a Catholic church, where a mass is held, during which the girl reaffirms her devotion to the church. Sometimes, a priest blesses a bible, rosary, or ring that is then given to the girl as a keepsake. After the mass, the girl's family hosts a great party. The girl is escorted by a male friend and wears a full-length gown. She is also attended by fourteen girls in similar dresses and their dates. The fifteen couples represent the girl's fifteen years of life. At the climax of the celebration, the teenagers are presented to the crowd and then dance an elaborately choreographed waltz.

In Cuba, *quinces* were held only by upper-class families. In the United States, however, less wealthy families began observing the ceremonies. Cuban American party planner Aurelio Nodarse told the *New York Times* in 1996 that he had "a lot of clients you wouldn't expect to be spending this kind of money—factory workers, an auto body shop manager. They save up for years for their daughters. It's a big deal." In Miami, *quinces* now fund a multimillion-dollar industry, employing caterers, dress designers, photographers, and bands. According to Nodarse, the average cost of a *quince* ranges from $8,000 to $50,000.

---

welcoming her family, even though they were the first Cubans ever to live in their small Indiana community:

> We found that the children in town were really curious about our family, the Cuban family that had arrived in town. I don't think that they knew what to expect. But they were always very helpful. They took us under their wings, and I was invited to all the kids' houses in town—to see what I looked like, I imagine. They helped me to learn English. They would come to our house the first week we were there and see what we were eating, if we wore shoes, if we knew how to use the phone, and if there was anything we needed.[36]

Although many missed the Cuban community in Miami, resettlement also helped give some immigrants a fresh start. For example, Manuel Alvarez, a Cuban exile who settled in Union City, New Jersey, in 1962, believed moving far from Miami helped him adapt to his new country:

Because so many Cubans settled in southwestern Miami, the area became known as Little Havana.

Those that came to Miami only heard the propaganda [that they would soon be able to move back to Cuba]. Those that came to the North had a much more open perspective. I think the reality of feeling a different kind of weather and having to bundle up gives you more time to reflect and makes you realize that the world is more than Cuba.[37]

Little Havana

The majority of exiles, however, still felt that living in Miami was the next best thing to living in Cuba. They chose to set down roots with other Cubans in a neighborhood in southwestern Miami. Because so many Cubans settled in this small area, it became known as Little Havana.

At the heart of Little Havana was Eighth Street, known to the Cuban immigrants by its Spanish name, Calle Ocho. In the early 1960s Cuban families began to pool their resources to open small businesses along this street. They cleaned boarded-up storefronts and hung handpainted signs announcing the opening of shops, restaurants, bakeries, and other small businesses.

Each time a new business opened on Calle Ocho, the Cuban community celebrated. The exiles were excited to be able to buy Cuban foods—such as *café con leche* (Cuban coffee with milk) and *arroz con pollo* (chicken with rice)—and other familiar goods that were generally unavailable elsewhere in the city. Each new store or shop also represented a small victory for their larger mission. The businesses stood as concrete evidence of the Cubans' ability to build successful lives in their new country.

The Entrepreneurial Spirit

Many of the early exiles had worked in business before they left Cuba, and now they applied their entrepreneurial skills once again. Some Cubans, however, decided to work for themselves only after they were unable to find other good jobs. The construction and garment industries were especially important fields for these workers. Working out of old pickup trucks, Cuban men, even recent immigrants with a limited knowledge of English, were able to scrounge for small construction jobs. Women with no previous work experience could do piecemeal sewing jobs at home for garment factories.

Frequently, people working these fields became subcontractors. A construction worker would sign a contract with a client to do a big job, then hire his friends to help out. Similarly, a seamstress might agree to deliver a large amount of sewing work to her employer and ask other Cuban women to her home to assist her in finishing the job. Some of the most successful subcontractors went on to own their own contracting businesses or garment factories.

Professionals, such as doctors, dentists, and architects, also started their own practices in Little Havana. Because they were not yet licensed to practice their professions in the United States, these were illegal businesses. Their clients were other Cubans who could be trusted not to report the owners to the authorities. This underground network of businesses helped many poor Cubans obtain needed services, because they could offer the owners services in lieu of money. For instance, a plumber might fix a doctor's sink in exchange for a physical exam.

This informal economic network helped unite the Cuban community. The exiles could purchase from one another almost every product or service they needed, often at a lower price than it would otherwise cost. Exile Mercedes Sandoval explained how this system worked:

> If I needed a roofer, well, I went to a buddy of mine who's from my hometown, and he's sure to give me a discount to have me as a client; of course, he'll charge me much less than an "American" would, but will still make some money. After a while, "Americans" involved in many of the trades and services started to leave because they simply couldn't compete.[38]

Cubans often worked and did business with non-Cubans, but because of the self-sufficiency of Little Havana, they generally did so by choice, not necessity.

Making Little Havana

The Cubans' economic network also helped Little Havana grow. Most Cubans who wanted to start businesses had to borrow money because Castro had confiscated all their savings and possessions. But without any assets to put up as collateral, most immigrants found that banks would not give them loans. Would-be business owners had to turn to the few Cubans who had jobs working in banking in Miami. These Cuban bankers were willing to lend to people whose friends and family would vouch for their good character. This access to capital, limited though it was, provided Little Havana the means to grow rapidly.

With its rapid growth, Little Havana became more than just an ethnic neighborhood. It became a near re-creation of the Cuba the exiles remembered. Blocks of Calle Ocho were soon lined with restaurants, bookstores, flower shops, clothing stores, and supermarkets. Many of these establishments took on the names of similar businesses in Cuba. If immigrants stayed in Little Havana, they could almost pretend that they had never been torn from their homeland. As writer Gustavo Pérez Firmat explained,

> An individual who lived [in Little Havana] could be delivered by a Cuban obstetrician, buried by a Cuban under-

A Cuban economic network in Miami allowed would-be business owners to open up restaurants and shops in Little Havana.

Celebrating *Nochebuena*

In his memoirs Next Year in Cuba, *Cuban American writer Gustavo Pérez Firmat described how his family revived in Miami the traditional Cuban celebration of* Nochebuena, *held on Christmas Eve.*

When we got to Miami in October 1960, we stopped celebrating Nochebuena. It seemed pointless to observe this feast in exile, with our unsettled situation and the family scattered all over—some relatives still in Cuba and others in New York and Puerto Rico. . . . My parents kept hoping that we would be back in Cuba in time to celebrate Nochebuena the way we always had, but it didn't happen. . . . Sitting around the table on Christmas Day, we weren't so much gloomy as dazed. We had been living in this house only a few weeks, everything was topsy-turvy, it wasn't clear what we were supposed to think or say. . . .

After a few years, our family reinstituted Nochebuena. By the late sixties everybody in our family had left Cuba, and if they didn't live in Miami, they were able to come down for Christmas. Since the family had been brought together again, it no longer felt [it was] inappropriate to celebrate in exile. Indeed, the opposite thing happened: distance from the homeland made us celebrate the occasion all the more vigorously, for Nochebuena became one of the ways of holding on to Cuba. Although the Nochebuenas in exile were less splendid than the Cuban ones, the essentials remained the same. During these years Little Havana was full of Cuban markets that carried all the typical foods. . . . If a family didn't have the time or the equipment to roast a pig at home, an already-cooked pig could be bought at the corner *bodega* [store], along with containers of *congrí* [rice and beans] and *yuca* [a potato-like vegetable]. . . . We went to church, pigged out on roast pork, and drank and danced.

---

taker, and in between birth and death lead a perfectly satisfactory life without needing extramural contacts. Little Havana was a golden cage, an artificial paradise, the neighborhood of dreams.[39]

Family Life

In their homes, the Cuban exiles also did all they could to re-create the world they used to know. In Cuba, the family was the most important social institution. Parents and children often shared their homes with grandparents and other relatives. During their first years in the United States, many family members and even several families lived together by necessity, because they were too poor to afford separate dwellings. But as their financial situation improved, relatives still wanted to stay close, even if they did not remain in the same home. One large, prosperous family, for instance, bought ten acres

It is important to Cuban Americans to preserve their culture and pass on traditions to their children.

of land, on which family members built ten houses so they could all live close by.

Following Cuban tradition, families gathered frequently for special meals and celebrations. Many shared a huge Sunday lunch featuring favorite Cuban foods, such as rice and beans, fried plantains, and *arroz con pollo* (a dish with chicken and rice). The most spectacular spread was reserved for *Nochebuena* (good night), the Cuban celebration of Christmas Eve. The centerpiece of the feast was a roast pig, which was usually carefully prepared by the men in the family. The exiles also adapted the American holiday of Thanksgiving as a celebration of thanks for their own safe delivery from communist Cuba. During their Thanksgiving dinner, families often raised their glasses to the toast, "Next year in Cuba," to reaffirm their dream of returning to the old country.

Fearing their children would forget about Cuba, adults became determined to preserve their culture. According to Professor Mercedes Sandoval, "The older parents, the grandparents, were instrumental in trying to conserve among the young generation the language as well as the Cuban music, the taste for Cuban culture and so forth."[40] To keep Cuba alive in the younger generation's imagination, parents and grandparents repeatedly told the children stories about their lives there. Exile groups organized classes in Cuban history and literature to instill in young people pride in the island's culture. Many families insisted on speaking Spanish among themselves; parents often corrected their children if at home they used the English they were learning in school.

The exiles' longing for Cuba also influenced the entertainment they favored. Cuban entertainers performed live shows with titles such as *Añorada Cuba* (Yearning for Cuba) and *La Cuba de Ayer* (Yesterday's Cuba). The most popular live performers, such as singers Celia Cruz and Olga Guillot, were those who had already been well known in the days before Castro. Spanish-language radio stations brought back memories as well by playing old Cuban songs. These stations and Spanish-language newspapers were also a source of the news that mattered most to the exiles—news from the island. Gustavo Pérez Firmat described the importance these reports had for Cuban families:

> Inside our house [in Miami], the radio was always tuned to one of the Cuban stations. . . . All we wanted was to hear about Cuba. Reports from the island were our life's blood. . . . Each day brought new signs of the Revolution's deterioration. There would be rumors of an uprising outside the capital. . . . These rumors swept across Little Havana like hurricane gusts. Someone would call our house with a news flash and my father would in turn call his friends and relatives.[41]

The Camarioca Boatlift

The exiles' ties to the island were also strengthened by a steady trickle of new immigrants. Despite the suspension of flights between Havana and Miami following the missile crisis, between October 1962 and September 1965, nearly fifty-eight thousand Cubans managed to make their way to America. Although most traveled to the United States via a third country, several thousand risked their lives by traveling by water across the Straits of Florida in small boats.

Cubans flee to the United States in a rickety homemade boat.

This trickle of immigration swelled briefly when in September 1965, Castro made a surprise announcement that any Cubans who wanted to join relatives in the United States would be allowed to leave the country. Castro's motives in easing exit restrictions were unclear. In any case, within hours, Cuban exiles were sending telegrams to Cuba, requesting exit permits for their relatives.

A refugee worker helps Cuban immigrants fill out paperwork to enter the United States.

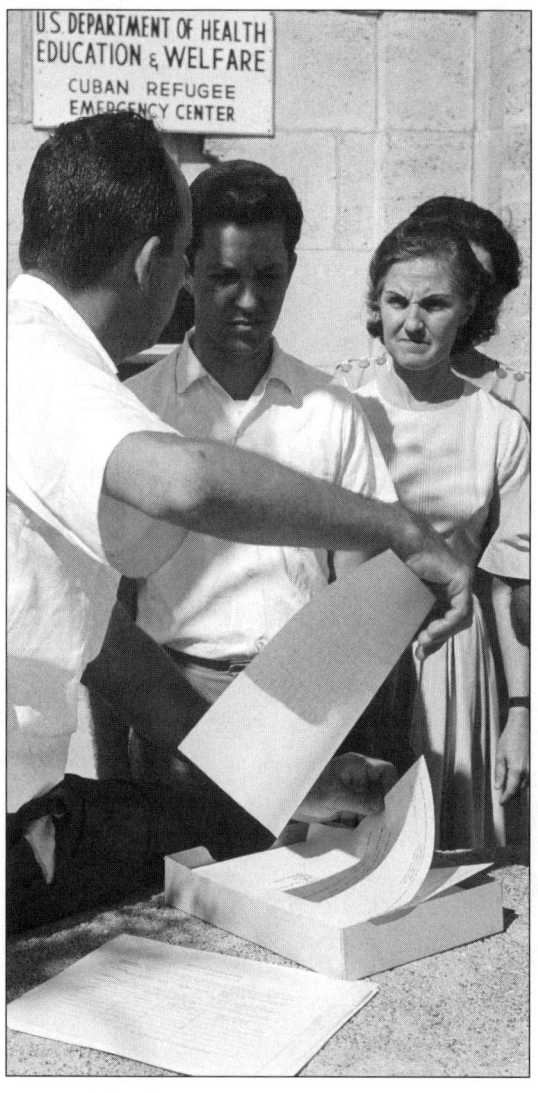

Castro declared that the exiles could pick up their relatives at Camarioca, a port on Cuba's northern coast. Immediately, Cubans left the Florida shore in hundreds of small boats. Some too rickety to make the trip soon broke down or began to sink. The U.S. Coast Guard saved the passengers of dozens of stranded boats. In a few cases, the people in troubled vessels were not so lucky and drowned. About five thousand Cubans made it to the United States before November 1965, when Castro responded to international pressure by calling off the Camarioca Boatlift.

The Freedom Flights

Immigration soon resumed in a more orderly way when the United States signed a Memorandum of Understanding with Cuba. Under the agreement, two flights would leave each day from Varadero, a town north of Havana. Officially known as Family Reunification Flights, they were soon dubbed "Freedom Flights" by the American press. President Lyndon Johnson made clear that the new immigrants were welcome, announcing that "the people of Cuba . . . who seek refuge here in America will find it. . . . Our tradition as an asylum for the oppressed is going to be upheld."[42]

Close relatives—spouses, parents, and children—of Cubans living in the United States were given the first priority for seats on the Freedom Flights. Men between the ages of seventeen and twenty-six, however, were generally not allowed to leave because they were eligible to serve in the Cuban army. Sometimes the Cuban Refugee Program was able to alert Cuban exiles already in Miami when their relatives were cleared to leave. But often relatives showed up in Miami with no warning. The erratic system often left the exiles on edge as they awaited reunions with their loved ones. Many anxiously listened to daily broadcasts on Spanish-language radio stations, during which the names of the day's expected arrivals were read.

For would-be immigrants, the waiting game was even more excruciating. To take a Freedom Flight, a Cuban first had to apply for an exit permit. Often applicants faced a long wait before they were permitted to board a plane. As soon as people asked to leave Cuba, they generally lost their jobs, which meant that they faced months or even years with no way to earn money to buy food. As a punishment, some were forced to work in government-owned fields at very low wages, sometimes for months or even years.

The Freedom Flight immigrants came from somewhat different backgrounds than the Golden Exiles. Unlike many of the earlier immigrants, the Freedom Flight immigrants were largely from the middle class. Many were owners of small businesses or skilled laborers, whose property and businesses had only recently been confiscated by Castro. The two waves of exiles also had different experiences as they set foot in the United States. When the Golden Exiles arrived, they had to say good-bye to the Cuba they loved; but thanks to their efforts, the Freedom Flight immigrants could settle in Cuban enclaves that were virtual re-creations of pre-Castro Cuba. For these immigrants, arriving in Little Havana was like going back in time.

CHAPTER FIVE

Becoming Cuban American

During the eight years the Freedom Flights operated, another three hundred thousand Cubans arrived in Miami. While nearly half settled in other areas of the United States, particularly in the burgeoning New York–Union City enclave, the rest chose to remain in southern Florida. This influx alarmed many non-Cubans in the area. They could not imagine how Miami could absorb so many new immigrants so quickly.

But instead of increasing unemployment and crime, these newcomers allowed Little Havana to flourish. As the Golden Exiles became more established, they prospered and expanded their businesses. The Freedom Flight immigrants provided a steady stream of cheap labor that helped these Cuban-owned businesses grow even more. And with the help of earlier immigrants, the new arrivals soon began opening their own businesses, creating still more jobs.

The financial success of the Cuban exiles not only benefited their neighborhoods, but also Miami as a whole. María Christina Herrera, the former director of the Institute of Cuban Studies, described how beginning in the 1970s, these and other Cuban-run enterprises helped transform the city:

> Although the Cuban refugee programme allocated millions of dollars

to initially help the Cubans, the Cubans have more than repaid those millions through taxes and through the development of the area, which was a sleepy winter tourist place. So greater Miami has become, primarily because of the Cubans, the centre of international finance and tourism and trade in the southern part of the U.S.[43]

The Financial Boom

Thanks to the hard work of the Golden Exiles and those who arrived aboard the Freedom Flights, Little Havana saw its greatest period of financial growth in the early 1970s. Ironically, a downturn in the national economy in 1973–74 worked to the advantage of many Cuban entrepreneurs. As the economy weakened, many larger businesses owned by non-Cubans closed down. Smaller Cuban-owned businesses moved in to take their place and thrived as the economy recovered. By the end of the 1970s, more than one-third of Miami's businesses were owned by Cuban immigrants.

At the same time, many Cuban professionals who had been providing services illegally to their neighbors finally obtained the necessary licenses to practice openly. In addition, the children of the Golden Exiles began graduating from colleges and universities with their own professional degrees. Many of the early immigrants sacrificed and saved to make sure their children could receive the best education possible.

Many immigrants sacrificed and saved to ensure a good education for their children.

Working Women

One of the primary reasons Cuban families found financial success in the United States was "women's work." In Cuba, most of women in the first waves of exiles had been housewives. But in the United States, they had to ignore tradition and take jobs outside the home if their families were to prosper. Leaving their children in the care of grandparents, many found work as waitresses, maids, seamstresses, factory workers, and vegetable pickers. Often, they held these jobs until the family had saved enough money to open a business, where they then worked alongside their husbands, older children, and other family members. Even after their families were financially secure, many women chose to stay in the workforce. By the 1980s the percentage of women in the Cuban American community holding jobs was higher than that of any other ethnic group.

They knew from experience that, while people could lose their money and possessions, an education was something no one, not even Castro, could take away.

Adding further to Little Havana's boom were hundreds of import-export businesses started by Cubans. These entrepreneurs traveled through Central and South America collecting orders for American goods. Here the Cubans' intimate knowledge of the cultures of Spanish-speaking countries paid off handsomely. Cuban businesspeople had the advantage of knowing from their own experience what types of goods their clients were most interested in. As these businesses thrived, Miami became known as the gateway to Latin America, overtaking New Orleans as the leading American city in trade with Latin American and Caribbean nations.

Coming Home

As Little Havana thrived, many Cuban immigrants who had settled elsewhere decided to relocate to Miami. So dramatic was this migration that by the end of the 1970s, about 40 percent of Cubans living in Miami came not directly from Cuba, but from elsewhere in the United States. Many of those who moved to Little Havana did so to reexperience the Cuba they remembered from their youth in Little Havana's shops and restaurants. Others too young to remember living in Cuba were drawn to Miami because the Cuban enclave there resembled what their parents had told them about the old country. Dario Moreno, a professor, spoke of his excitement when he moved to Miami:

> From the moment I arrived in [Miami], I knew I had returned to the Cuba that my parents had always described to me when I was a kid growing up in Los Angeles. They always talked about Cuba with such love that anyone would have had to be completely heartless not to want to buy in.

And Miami is the only place where the Cuba they loved and taught me to love still exists. . . . As a Cuban, I just feel at home in Miami in a way that I don't anywhere else in the world that I've lived in.[44]

The Cuban enclave also attracted people from elsewhere in Latin America. Businesspeople, tourists, and immigrants from other Spanish-speaking nations such as Peru and Venezuela flocked to Little Havana. There they found food, music, and other elements of Hispanic culture that they could not find in most other American cities.

The New Cuban Americans

In the late 1960s and early 1970s, a new generation of Cuban immigrants came of age. Growing up in the United States, with their parents preoccupied with building a new life, many children experienced much more independence than they would have in Cuba. As one immigrant recalled,

> Exile had brought me a special kind of freedom. At Dade Elementary, for the first and only time in our lives, my brother Pepe and I walked to school. After school, we went home and I headed for the park or the Boy's Club, where I stayed until nightfall. In Cuba

Many Cuban immigrants moved to Little Havana to reexperience the Cuban environment of their youth.

no kid in my family was allowed to walk to school, much less roam the streets. In fact, most things public were off limits to us in Havana. . . . Once in the United States, within certain limits, we were on our own and we made the most of it.[45]

Leaving Cuba as children and young adults, this generation was also old enough to remember the pre-Castro days but young enough to have grown up influenced by American culture. While many of their parents continued to dream of their return to Cuba, this younger generation had come to think of the United States as home, especially as they started families in their adopted country. They were comfortable thinking of themselves as Cuban Americans, not just Cubans who happened to be living in America.

As these Cuban Americans reached their twenties and thirties, they began having a greater influence on Little Havana and other Cuban enclaves. They developed a hybrid culture that incorporated both American and Cuban ways. Performers such as Willy Chiriro made new music influenced by American pop instead of singing the nostalgic Cuban songs that had earlier dominated Spanish-language radio. Cuban American artists such as Rafael So-

A woman walks past a mural in Little Havana that incorporates both American and Cuban cultures.

Younger Cuban Americans, though still in touch with their culture, focus on their future in the United States.

riano painted in contemporary styles, and Cuban American authors such as Gustavo Pérez Firmat wrote, often in English, about their experiences in the United States. Many young Cuban American businesspeople and professionals became comfortable working and living alongside non-Cubans. They were often called YUCAs (Young Urban Cuban Americans)—the name a play on yuca, a vegetable used in many traditional Cuban dishes.

For the YUCAs and their contemporaries, Cuba's past loomed much less important than it had for their parents. While many of the older generation still looked back in time, wishing to return to the Cuba of pre-Castro days, these younger Cuban Americans focused on their future in the United States. In the mid-1960s, 83 percent of Cuban Americans said they would go back to the island if they could. Only a decade later, just 30 percent said they had an interest in returning.

Despite the growing tensions between the generations, many younger Cuban Americans still embraced aspects of traditional Cuban life, particularly the values taught to them by their parents, such as the importance of family and of getting a good education. And despite their commitment to life as Americans, most wanted older family members to share memories of Cuba with the younger generations. One of the Golden Exiles, Irma de Leon, recounted how her daughter encouraged her to talk about life on the island to her grandchildren: "My daughter always said, 'When the children come to your home, speak to them about Cuba, tell them about Cuba, because I want them to know they are part Cuban and part American, that we are proud and have a lot of things to be proud of."[46]

Protest and Terrorism

And even as Cuban Americans became more involved in American life, the politics of Cuba remained for them an important issue. Many grew frustrated as the U.S. government focused its foreign policy on Vietnam, where it was sending U.S. troops to fight communist guerrillas. Cuban Americans felt the United States should be battling what they perceived as the threat communism posed far closer to home, in Castro's Cuba.

To revive attention to Cuba's plight, Cuban Americans began staging public protests. Several student groups, such as the Federation of Cuban Students and Abdala, were particularly active. In 1971 sixteen members of Abdala made news by chaining themselves to the United Nations Building in New York during a protest rally. The next year five thousand Cuban Americans marched on Washington, D.C., to show their anger at President Richard M. Nixon's plan to visit Cuba's communist ally, the Soviet Union.

A few Cuban Americans even resorted to violence as a means of bringing attention to their cause. Between 1973 and 1976, radical anti-Castro groups exploded more than one hundred bombs in south Florida. Their targets were both officials in Castro's government and Cuban Americans whom they branded as traitors for wanting to open communications between the United States and Cuba. The violence culminated in 1976, when a bomb blew up a Cubana de Aviación airplane off the coast of Barbados, killing seventy-three passengers. Some Cuban American extremists supported this terrorism. Expressing their views, one journalist wrote, "The realities of world politics leave no alternative but to use violence. Only when the exiles destroy the lives and interests of our enemies will Washington, Moscow, the OAS [Organization of American States], or whoever take our views into account."[47] The vast majority of Cuban Americans, however, found such terrorist tactics repugnant. By the mid-1970s, they embraced a nonviolent means of bringing attention to the issues most important to them by becoming involved in American politics.

Getting Out the Vote

To the first Cuban exiles, politics in the United States had seemed irrelevant because they had expected Castro to be overthrown, allowing them to return to Cuba. Also, as Cuban citizens, they did not have the right to vote in the United States, making it difficult for them to have much influence over American politicians. In large measure, these earlier immigrants were comfortable with that state of affairs. Even after the Cuban Adjustment Act of 1966 made it easier for Cubans to obtain U.S. citizenship, few were interested in doing so because American citizenship required pledging allegiance to the United States—a pledge that many Cuban Americans saw as a sign of disloyalty to Cuba. Some immigrants who wanted to become U.S. citizens chose not to because they did not want to earn the contempt of their friends and neighbors.

By the 1970s, however, some Cuban Americans started wanting more of a voice in Miami's local politics. Among them were Manolo Reboso and Alfredo Durán. Both were highly respected in the Cuban American community for their participation in the 1961 Bay of Pigs invasion. Although not enough Cuban American voters existed to elect officials from their own ranks, there were enough to make it worth the while of non-Cuban candidates to court the Cuban American vote. Reboso and Durán escorted candidates who pledged to help Cuban Americans to Little Havana. At political rallies, the candidates declared their desire to see a Castro-free Cuba to loud cheers and applause. Even though these candidates—if elected—could do little to affect U.S. policy toward Cuba, Cuban Americans appreciated this show of support. And being able to deliver the votes from Little Havana earned the Cuban Americans their first posts in city government: Reboso was appointed to the City of Miami Commission, and Durán was appointed to the Dade County School Board.

Even as their influence grew, Cuban Americans still lacked the popularity outside of Little Havana to be elected to office themselves. If Cuban Americans were to win local elections, more Cuban American voters were needed. In pursuit of this goal, politically savvy Cuban Americans established citizenship and voter registration drives. Still, older Cuban exiles worried that becoming a U.S. citizen would make them

To win local elections, Cuban immigrants needed to establish citizenship.

appear disloyal to Cuba. To overcome this objection, the Cuban Americans running the citizenship drives appealed to the exiles' Cuban patriotism. They explained that the best way to affect U.S. policy toward Cuba was to vote for candidates who promised to oppose Castro. In part because of these vigorous efforts, the number of Cuban American voters doubled in the 1970s, making them a force that could no longer be ignored in Miami politics.

The Dialogue

As Cuban Americans began flexing their muscle on the local political front, some also started reconsidering the old hard-line stance against Castro. Older exiles agreed with U.S. policy, which was aimed at isolating Castro by cutting off all diplomatic and trade ties with Cuba. A few young Cuban Americans, however, began questioning whether opening talks between Castro and the United States might be the best hope for Cuba. The U.S. refusal to trade with Cuba had nearly destroyed the island's economy, they suggested, and caused many ordinary Cubans to suffer severe shortages of food and other necessities.

Among those who believed in more communication with Castro were members of the Antonio Maceo Brigade—college students who named their organization after one of the leaders of the Cuban revolution of 1895. In 1977 Castro surprised the students by inviting them to tour Cuba. Afterward, the organization members told others of the experiences on the island, hoping to encourage more contact with Castro: "We gave interviews about the trip, we gave talks about it, we gave slide-shows to interested youngsters, we gave talks in the university and contributed in whatever way possible at the time for the normalisation of relations between Cuba and the United States."[48] Although condemned as dangerous radicals by many Cuban Americans, the Antonio Maceo Brigade made two more trips to the island in 1978 and 1979.

On September 6, 1978, Castro held a press conference attended by several Cuban American journalists. There, he announced what he called his Dialogue Policy, declaring his willingness to discuss with Cuban exiles the relationship between the United States and Cuba. Two months later, he hosted seventy-five exiles at the Dialogue Conference. As a result of these talks, Castro agreed to several concessions important to the exiles in attendance. He announced he would release more than thirty-five hundred political prisoners, most of whom had been confined in Cuba for almost twenty years. Castro also promised to let Cuban Americans return to Cuba for week-long visits with relatives.

Many Cuban Americans were suspicious of Castro's motives. They claimed that the prisoner release was merely an attempt to improve Castro's reputation, which had suffered from accusations that he violated human rights. They also suspected that allowing visitors was a calculated move designed to shore up the foundering Cuban economy with U.S. dollars. Some Cuban Americans believed as well that Castro was trying to drive a wedge into their community, by pitting those who wanted a more open relationship with Cuba against those who did not.

Lourdes Casal

In the 1970s writer and scholar Lourdes Casal became a leading force among Cuban Americans seeking a more open relationship with the Cuban government. Casal was born in Havana in 1938. As a girl, she proved herself a talented student in public and private schools. She attended Havana's Catholic University for seven years, where she studied psychology.

In college, Casal became involved in several student groups that supported Fidel Castro's revolutionary 26th of July Movement. When Castro led a successful revolution in Cuba in 1959, she was among his many supporters. But as Castro began embracing communism, Casal began speaking out against his reforms. As a known member of the underground anti-Castro movement, Casal had to flee the island in 1961. The following year, she settled in New York City and continued her studies at the New School for Social Research. She received her doctorate in 1975.

In addition to her scholarly writing, Casal published *El Caso Padilla,* a collection of documents about the growing tensions between Cuba's intellectuals and Castro's government. She also helped found the Institute of Cuban Studies and *Areito,* a literary magazine dedicated to Cuban culture. Unlike the majority of Cuban American scholars, Casal, though critical of Castro, saw some merits in his reforms, particularly those that aided the poor. Because of this stance, the Cuban government invited her to visit the island in 1973. She soon returned to participate in a conference at the University of Havana. Wanting other Cuban Americans to have the chance to see modern-day Cuba, she helped create the Antonio Maceo Brigade, a moderate student political group whose members were permitted to tour the island in 1977.

Knowing she was terminally ill from a kidney ailment, Casal returned to Cuba in 1979. She died there two years later. Although her pro-Castro positions did not reflect the sentiments of most Cuban Americans, she was a powerful force in the community's changing political landscape in the 1970s.

Whatever Castro's actual intentions might have been, the Dialogue certainly caused dissension between the two factions. Tensions ran high as the anti-Castro faction denounced the Dialogue participants. Many who favored dialogue with Castro became the targets of harassment, and two, Eulalio José Negrín and Carlos Muñis Varela, were assassinated.

The Blue Jeans Revolution

Cuban Americans who decided to visit Cuba under the new policy were also criticized by the most rabid opponents of Castro. An editorial in one Cuban American newspaper asserted, "It is sad to see Cubans today, supposedly exiles, giving money to the regime that humiliated them years ago and is now humiliating them by forcing them to return to their homeland as tourists."[49] Those who journeyed to Cuba knew they were taking some risks: In choosing to travel to Cuba, Cuban Americans not only earned the ill will of their neighbors. They also feared that they could be trapped in the country if Castro decided to detain them.

Still, many Cuban Americans felt they had to take advantage of this opportunity to be reunited with loved ones they had not seen for decades. Some wanted to see elderly parents, possibly for the last time. Others were eager to introduce their children to relatives they had known only through photographs.

For some, returning to their homeland proved a difficult experience. Cuba was now a poor and struggling country, with little in common with the beautiful, vibrant island enshrined in popular memory. Seeing long-lost relatives again was also sometimes hard. Magdalena Garcia, who had arrived in the United States in 1967 at the age of ten, described meeting relatives after a twelve-year absence: "I remembered all my family, lots of neighbors and people. It was like going back to a different world. The people—even

---

Our Lady of Charity

In 1973 Our Lady of Charity first opened its doors to the Cuban Americans of Miami. Named after Cuba's patron saint, the Catholic Church has served ever since as the spiritual center of Cubans in exile. Every year, more than one hundred thousand Catholics make a pilgrimage to the church.

Our Lady of Charity was the dream of Father Agustin Roman, a Cuban priest who emigrated to Miami in 1966. For years he collected contributions for its construction from Cuban exiles, many of whom were struggling just to put food on their tables. Roman once recalled, "We asked people to contribute an hour's wages every week. I personally carried $30,000 [worth of] pennies to the bank."

Built along the shores of Biscayne Bay, Our Lady of Charity faces the waters that separate Miami from Cuba. The structure is full of symbolism. The rough pews are reminiscent of those used long ago by workers on Cuba's sugar plantations. Its six rafters represent the six provinces into which Cuba was traditionally divided. A stone beneath the altar was made of sand from all six provinces mixed with water taken from a raft on which fifteen Cubans died while trying to sail to the United States. Behind the altar is a mural by exile artist Teok Carrasco that depicts people and events in Cuban history.

In a *USA Today* article published on January 21, 1998, Father Jose Nickse explained the important role Our Lady of Charity had played in the lives of many Cuban immigrants: "The shrine is a very, very sacred place. For many who come from Cuba, the first thing they do is visit. First they pray for having gotten out, and then they pray for families left behind."

though they still know it's you, they look at you under a different light; you're a different person now."⁵⁰

The meetings also had a profound effect on the visitors' Cuban relatives. For years, Castro had told the Cuban people that their exiled relatives were "worms" and "scum." But meeting these supposed traitors face to face left many Cubans with a very different impression. Mirta Ojito, who grew up in Castro's Cuba, described how visiting with Cuban American relatives when she was a teenager made her question Castro's rule for the first time:

> Meeting my family from America, seeing that they were nice people and not traitors, and hearing their stories of hard work and long days—but also of great rewards—marked a turning point in my life. Disappointed with the lies and hypocrisies of the regime and tired of seeing my parents work and struggle in vain, I told my father I was ready to go with him to the United States when the time came.⁵¹

In the end, the Dialogue Policy proved a miscalculation for Castro. Like Ojito, few Cubans could ignore the concrete evidence of the prosperity of the Cuban American visitors. One journalist wrote,

> [At a] time when most Cubans were asked to tighten their belts and face more years of hard work for little return, relatives from Miami and New Jersey were flooding back into the country with tales of the good life in the U.S. To hear them tell it, everyone had a mansion, three cars, an unlimited number of TV sets, and more food than anyone could eat.⁵²

Those who returned to Cuba were met by a poor and struggling country, nothing like the beautiful island of popular memory.

Visitors showered relatives with toys, radios, stereo equipment, and televisions, but possibly the most welcome gift was a pair of blue jeans. Many young Cubans took to wearing these American-made jeans as an emblem of their anger at Castro for lying to them about conditions in the United States. The visits, therefore, prompted a new movement in Cuba, which became known as the blue jeans revolution. The so-called revolution was fueled not only by a newfound contempt for Castro, but also by the desire of many Cubans to live the good life the United States now seemed to offer.

BECOMING CUBAN AMERICAN 73

CHAPTER SIX

The Marielitos

In 1980 the Cuban American community was faced with one of its greatest challenges—absorbing a great third wave of Cuban immigrants, who later became known as the Marielitos. The story of the Marielitos began on April 1, when six Cubans crashed a stolen bus through the gates of the Peruvian embassy in Havana. They knew that the Peruvian government had granted asylum to other Cubans who had recently managed to enter the embassy compound and that these people had subsequently been allowed to move to Peru. To many miserable Cubans, the embassy therefore came to represent their last hope of ever escaping Cuba.

As the bus entered the embassy compound, Cuban guards outside opened fire. Two of the people on the bus were injured, and one of the guards was accidentally killed in the shooting. Castro angrily demanded that the Peruvian ambassador turn over the gate-crashers. The ambassador refused, and in retaliation, Castro removed his guards from the outside of the embassy compound, leaving it open to anyone who wanted to enter.

Word spread throughout Cuba that the embassy's gates were open. Within days, almost eleven thousand people converged on the compound, all hoping to leave the country with the Peruvian embassy's help. Rustino Ferra, a Cuban employee of the embassy, described the chaotic scene: "Thousands of people came to the embassy. Some ran inside and stayed; others just came to see what was going on, then left. By nightfall, there was no space left inside. . . . Someone painted a huge sign to show the foreign press helicopters flying over the embassy. It said 'CUBA NO MORE.'"[53]

The compound became so full of people, no one could move. To get a little breathing room, some crawled up to the roof of the embassy building, but soon that space, too, was filled.

Peru itself would agree to take in only one thousand refugees, so the embassy scrambled to find temporary and permanent homes in other countries for the rest. The United States, Costa Rica, Spain, Ecuador, Argentina, and Canada all agreed to help by taking in some of these refugees. In the meantime, the crowd at the embassy refused to leave, even though they had almost no food and water. Photographs and stories of the hoards of people willing to starve to death for a chance to leave Cuba soon became international news.

Support for the Refugees

The incident galvanized Cuban Americans, who quickly rallied to lend their support. Some offered to stage an invasion, according

Refugees leave the Peruvian Embassy under police protection. Almost eleven thousand Cubans sought asylum when the embassy's gates opened.

THE MARIELITOS

to Rafael Fernandez, a Cuban American from New York who was visiting Miami at the time: "The old militants came out of the woodwork and advocated one or another military remedy for the situation. Some people began to train troops. . . . You could have put a sign-up office on 8th Street and had 10,000 soldiers in a day!"[54] Other Cuban Americans sent telegrams to President Jimmy Carter, asking him to intervene in the crisis. Still others organized food and clothing drives. Spanish-language radio station WQBA asked for financial contributions and raised more than $100,000 in one day. These efforts, however, did little good: The Cuban government kept all of this aid from reaching the Cubans at the embassy.

Castro, bitter that the incident was reflecting badly on him, began denouncing those who wanted to leave Cuba. He called them delinquents and deviants and said they were to blame for all of Cuba's problems. In a speech delivered before an audience of 1 million Cubans, Castro declared that Cuba was lucky to be rid of these asylum seekers: "We say to those who do not have the genes of revolutionaries, or the blood of revolutionaries, or who do not have the necessary discipline and heroism for a revolution: we don't want you, we don't need you."[55]

Cubans who were still pro-Castro responded by gathering outside the embassy and jeering at the crowds waiting for asylum. Some threw stones and rotted foods. The po-

Before an audience of 1 million Cubans, Castro denounced the asylum seekers.

lice joined in, often beating up or siccing dogs on the people inside the embassy gates. Despite the harassment, most refused to leave. Finally, on April 16, the first airplanes arrived to take the emigrants out of Cuba.

The Mariel Boatlift

Four days later, Castro announced that anyone who wanted to do so was free to leave Cuba from Mariel, a small port twenty miles west of Havana. Castro probably reasoned that these people might rise against his regime if he forced them to stay in Cuba. Most likely, he also recognized other advantages to getting these people off the island. Cuba was then suffering from high unemployment rates and a severe housing shortage. Lowering the country's population would help solve both of these problems. As scholar Miguel Gonzalez-Pando explained,

> In the aftermath of exile visits and the Peruvian embassy crisis, mounting discontent among the island's population had reached such menacing levels that the Cuban leader was persuaded that the time had come to open the safety valve once more. In one bold sweep, he hoped to release internal pressures and defuse the volatile political situation on the island, while resolving the problem of the Peruvian embassy refugees.[56]

Within days of Castro's announcement, Cuban Americans set off from Key West in hundreds of boats, hoping to retrieve their friends and relatives. Some did not even have relatives left on the island but felt a duty to help any Cuban who wanted to escape Castro's rule. Many Cuban Americans spent their savings to charter boats for the trip across the Straits of Florida. Highway 1, the road that connects Miami to Key West, was clogged with traffic as people rushed to join what journalists dubbed the Freedom Flotilla.

The Mariel boatlift was unprecedented in its size and scope. The Camariorca boatlift of 1965 had lasted two months and brought five thousand immigrants to the United States. The Mariel boatlift would last five months and involve twenty-five times that number of people. Before Castro suspended the boatlift in September 1980, nearly 125,000 Cubans—1 percent of the country's population—would make their way to America.

Leaving Mariel

While the Freedom Flotilla headed toward Mariel, those Cubans who wanted to leave the island made their way to the port. Many had to wait for days for transportation to Mariel. In the meantime, they were harassed and beaten by Castro loyalists with the encouragement of the Cuban government. Mirta Ojito, then a high school student, later wrote about the terror in the streets:

> Mariel marked the first time socialist Cuba turned against itself. The government staged riots called *actos de repudio*—street rallies in which neighbors turned against neighbors, harassing and tormenting those who wanted to leave the country. The victims were often pelted with rocks, tomatoes, and eggs. Windows were shattered. Doors were

More than 125,000 Cuban refugees migrated to the United States during the Mariel boatlift of 1980.

knocked down. Some people were killed, dragged through the streets as trophies to intolerance and hate. Sometimes people trapped inside their homes chose to kill themselves rather than face their tormentors.[57]

The Marielitos found little relief once they reached Mariel, where crowds of Castro's supporters hurled stones and shouted insults, calling them traitors to the revolution. The scene was chaotic. Sometimes people spent weeks without food, frantically looking for their relatives in the hundreds of boats filling the waters. The harbor was so crowded that some joked that if the boats were laid end to end, they would stretch all the way back to Key West; the immigrants could then simply walk from boat to boat, all the way to the United States.

Desperate to get out of the port, Marielitos all too often crowded on to boats that could barely stay afloat even without the extra passengers. The overloading sometimes led to disaster. A witness recounted the sad fate of the passengers in one overcrowded vessel:

They ran into bad weather and a wave toppled them. Fourteen people died, I think, but many more have not been found [and are presumed dead]. Among the dead was an entire family—mother, father, two daughters, and a grandmother—who drowned. The only member of the family saved was a fourteen year old girl. . . . [The reports from Mariel] are all very sad stories that the world, I think, does not want to believe.[58]

The "Undesirables"

As thousands of people risked their lives to flee Cuba, Castro became alarmed that the Mariel boatlift was giving the world the impression that most Cubans wanted to leave their homeland. Eager to discredit the Marielitos, he called them "the scum of the country—antisocials, homosexuals, drug addicts, and gamblers."[59] To make his claims seem more valid, he forced criminals, mental patients, people with severe physical handicaps, and other Cubans he considered "undesirables" to join the exodus. As one

---

Excludable Aliens

Newspaper accounts of the Marielitos implied that many were violent felons. In fact, only a modest percentage of these immigrants had been jailed for serious crimes in Cuba. They and the small number of Marielitos who committed crimes once they arrived in the United States were classified as "excludable aliens." They were placed in prison and once they served their sentence, they were to be deported, or returned, to Cuba.

Castro, however, initially refused to let these criminals back into his country. As prisoners completed their sentences, the U.S. government confronted a dilemma: It could not deport the criminals, but it did not want to unleash them into American society either. The government chose to keep them in prison. By American law, "excludable aliens" had few rights. Legally, they could be detained as long as the government wished.

By 1987 more than two thousand excludable aliens were left in federal detention centers. Groups such as the Coalition to Support Cuban Detainees, Facts About Cuban Exiles, and the American Civil Liberties Union fought for their release. Expressing the views of many Marielito activists, Siro del Castillo of *Facts About Cuban Exiles* stated in the *New York Times* on April 14, 1990, "No one should be jailed for an indefinite period. And no one should be deported back to Cuba. It's just hypocritical for the United States to criticize Cuba for human rights violations and then deport people back there."

In November 1987, desperate Marielitos rioted in detention centers in Oakdale, Louisiana, and Atlanta, Georgia. After a lengthy standoff between the prisoners and police, the United States bowed to the Marielitos' demand that their cases be individually reviewed, a process that took several years. Eventually, Castro agreed to take back some of these Marielitos, but only about four hundred were ultimately deported to Cuba. The rest were allowed leave the detention centers and live in the United States.

Marielito, Mirta Ojito, noted, Cuban Americans manning boats were often compelled to take these people aboard along with their relatives:

> Not too long after our group boarded the boat, a bus stopped a few feet from the dock and people began pouring out. Some were shoeless; others wore orange uniforms that retained the creases of clothes that had been folded for too long; most had their heads shaved. A few were crying. They boarded [our boat], and the captain was instructed by Cuban immigration officers to take them to the United States.
>
> We did not know it then, but they were people that the Cuban government wanted to get rid of. Some were prisoners, doing time for crimes that ranged from theft to manslaughter. . . . By sending them abroad, the government was not only ridding itself of problems but also turning the Mariel crisis into Washington's problem.[60]

Some law-abiding people were so desperate to leave Cuba that they went to police and confessed to imaginary crimes and vices, hoping that they, too, would be loaded onto vessels bound for the United States. In one case, a government worker who had become disillusioned with Castro hastened his escape by asking his coworkers to write letters to the police full of lies about his antisocial behavior.

The U.S. Perspective

The nature and scope of the Mariel boatlift caught U.S. government policy makers off guard. Initially, President Carter had encouraged Americans to greet the Marielitos with open arms. But as their numbers increased and rumors of the criminals among them spread, the U.S. government was sent into a panic. The task of taking in so many immigrants in such a short amount of time was daunting, but short of a show of force, there was little the government could do to stop the Marielitos from heading to the United States.

The federal government did tell Cuban Americans to stop taking boats to Cuba and threatened them with heavy fines if they continued. The threats had little effect: Most Cuban Americans were so determined to be

Most Cuban Americans were willing to pay any price to be reunited with their relatives.

The Immigration and Naturalization Service was barraged with refugees during the Mariel boatlift. Tent cities were erected to accommodate the overflow.

reunited with their relatives that they were willing to pay any price. The boats stopped coming only when Castro ended the boatlift in September 1980.

As the Marielitos flooded into Miami, officials of the Immigration and Naturalization Service (INS) struggled to process the new immigrants. Some were quickly released into the custody of relatives. But many Marielitos had no family in the United States. By law, they had to be detained until sponsors could be found for them. Tens of thousands were placed in temporary housing in churches, gymnasiums, and recreational centers. Soon, tent cities were built in parks and underneath expressways to accommodate the overflow. The government even leased the Orange Bowl football stadium to house the growing number of homeless immigrants.

Dealing with the Marielitos

The INS also faced the difficult task of identifying the so-called undesirables among the Marielitos. The agency discovered that about twenty-six thousand—an alarming one-fifth of all the immigrants—had criminal records. But further investigation showed that the majority had been imprisoned for their political views or for minor infractions, such as stealing food. Others were jailed in Cuba for being alcoholics, gamblers, or homosexuals—behaviors that were not even regarded as criminal under U.S. federal law. In the end, only about five thousand—4 percent of the Marielitos—were found to have hard criminal records. Several thousand more immigrants were found to be suffering from mental illness.

Santería

Marielitos of African descent brought to the United States a new religion—Santería. Santería developed from the traditions of the Yoruba people of present-day Nigeria and Benin. From the sixteenth to the nineteenth century, Yoruba came to Cuba as slaves to work on sugar plantations.

Practitioners of Santería believe in a supreme being, known as Olorun or Olodumare, who interacts with humans through *orishas*—spirits who control the elements of nature and the daily lives of human beings. People who practice Santería are careful to perform proper rituals and make offerings to the *orishas,* believing that, if they do not, the *orishas* will punish them with illness or cause them other problems.

Santería associates each *orisha* with a different Catholic saint. The *orisha* Eleguá, for instance, is linked with Saint Peter, because both are thought to guard the gates of heaven. Yoruba slaves probably developed this system long ago out of necessity. Their masters expected them to convert to Catholicism. The Yoruba could appear to comply by praying to saints, when in fact they were honoring the *orishas* they revered.

The Marielitos were hardly the "scum" of Cuba, as Castro had claimed they were. Most were law-abiding citizens who consciously made the choice to come to the United States. In some ways, however, they differed from the earlier waves of Cuban immigrants. The immigrants of the 1960s and 1970s were largely from the middle and upper classes of Havana and other large cities. The Marielitos were more often from the lower class, though generally they were still more educated than the average Cuban. Some were from cities, but many were from the countryside.

Many of the first Cuban exiles had come to the United States as families. The Marielitos, on the other hand, were about 70 percent male. Many were young single men who had wanted to come to America on the Freedom Flights, but were forced to stay in Cuba to serve in Castro's army. The racial makeup of the Marielitos also distinguished them from earlier immigrants, most of whom were non-African. About 40 percent of the Marielitos were of full or mixed African ancestry.

Unlike the Cuban immigrants before them, the Marielitos had also spent many years living under communist rule. The youngest had never known any other system of government. For the Marielitos, moving to a democratic country was like coming to a new world—one where they had to adapt to a completely different way of working, living, and thinking.

A Bitter Welcome

Perhaps the greatest challenge faced by Marielitos, however, was overcoming prejudice. Sensational press accounts of Castro rounding up prisoners for the boatlift conveyed the idea that the average Marielito was a criminal. This stereotype was reinforced by television shows and movies, which routinely depicted recent Cuban immigrants as drug dealers and psychopaths.

Contempt for the Marielitos grew as their arrival led to a temporary rise in crime rates and unemployment in southern Florida. The government tried to relieve the situation by resettling the immigrants in other areas. But negative news reports about the Marielitos scared off many families and church groups who had earlier offered to sponsor them. Unable to place them with sponsors, the U.S. government continued to feed and house large numbers of Cubans, eventually spending more than $1 billion on the problem. In 1981, Marielito Estanislao Menendez described the frustration he and many other immigrants felt as they waited in the makeshift camps: "The irony of it all hits me every day when I wake up. I risked my life. For what? To gain freedom. *Libertad,* that's all I wanted. And here I am inside a compound surrounded by armed guards—not in jail, but not free. I can't find a sponsor. I don't know why. . . . Do they know we are here?"[61]

The Mariel boatlift created other problems for the Cuban American community in the form of a backlash against anyone of Cuban ancestry. In Miami-Dade County, a group of non-Spanish-speaking citizens proposed a referendum ending the county's policy of bilingualism. The policy, which called for all official documents and signs to be printed in English and Spanish, had been instituted in 1973 as a gesture of goodwill to the Cuban American community. Seven years later, a sizable majority of county residents voted to terminate the policy, an action intended by some voters to send a signal to their Cuban American neighbors. Despite their past success and achievements, all Cuban immigrants in the area would now be held in suspicion.

Old and New Immigrants

Initially, most Cuban Americans tried to help the Marielitos. Exile groups collected money for the new immigrants, which brought food and clothing to the refugee camps, and scrambled to find them sponsors and jobs. But when the negative attention given to the Marielitos began to tarnish the reputation of other Cuban Americans, some tried to disassociate themselves from recent immigrants. Older exiles were especially apt to make distinctions between "old" and "new" Cuban Americans.

Adding to their contempt for the Marielitos were old racial prejudices many exiles

The Marielitos waited in cramped makeshift camps for their freedom.

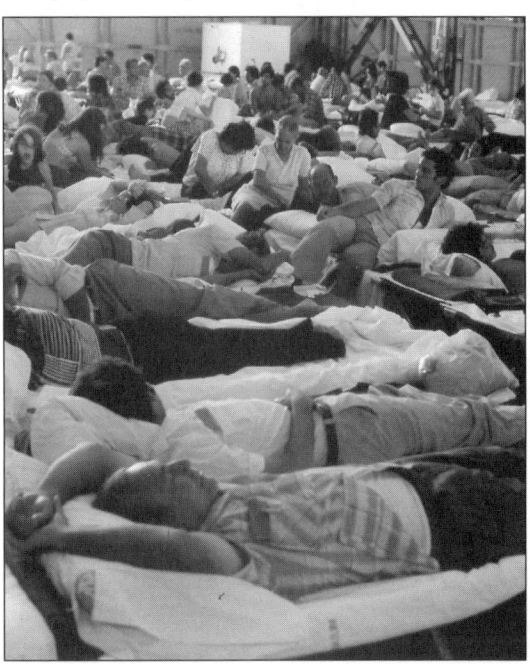

had learned in pre-Castro Cuba. Pedro Santa Cruz, an Afro-Cuban Marielito who settled in Washington, D.C., described how these prejudices stymied his attempt to find an apartment for his mother in Little Havana:

> When I started looking for an apartment, it hit me how racist the established Cuban community there was. I'd call and people would be pleasant on the telephone. "Yes, Mr. Santa Cruz, how nice, a Cuban from Washington. Please come over, have a look." And then we would show up, they would see that we were black, and suddenly the apartment wasn't available anymore.[62]

Despite the obstacles faced by the Marielitos, the majority adapted well to their new American life.

Marielito Pride

Despite the many obstacles the Marielitos faced, the majority adapted to American life with surprising ease. About 75 percent settled in the Miami area, many in the suburb of Hialeah, where rents were lower than in Little Havana. Instead of being a long-term drain on local social services as many Miamians feared, most Marielitos quickly found jobs. Although the majority did not experience the great financial success many Cuban immigrants had enjoyed in past years, Marielito workers were generally able to find a place for themselves in the local economy. Within a decade of arriving in the United States, the rate of unemployment among Marielitos was about the same as that of the general American population.

As the Marielitos adjusted to their new country, they became a significant influence on Cuban American life. For thirty years, most Cuban Americans had seen Castro as a near devil who had destroyed their homeland. The Marielitos, however, brought with them a more balanced view of Castro and his reforms. Although they acknowledged the failings of Castro's government, they also recognized he had made some changes that benefited Cuban society. For instance, his regime had ended some of the discrimination against black Cubans and helped the poor by increasing their access to health care and education. Reminded of the great social inequities that had existed under the Batista regime, some older immigrants were compelled to reexamine their romanticized vision of pre-Castro Cuba.

The Marielitos also made enormous contributions to the culture of their adopted

Reinaldo Arenas

Since his arrival in the United States on the 1980 Mariel boatlift, Reinaldo Arenas has emerged as one of the most important Cuban American writers. Arenas was born on July 16, 1943, near the town of Holguín in rural Cuba. Raised in poverty, he did not attend school until he was a teenager. At fifteen, Arenas joined the guerrilla force led by Fidel Castro, which staged a successful revolution in 1959.

After studying accounting and economic planning, Arenas began working as an assistant librarian at the Biblioteca Nacional José Martí (José Martí National Library) in Havana, while writing in his free time. In 1964 he began working on *Celestina antes del Alba,* a novel inspired by his impoverished youth. The book won several awards and was published in Cuba in 1967. It was Arenas's only novel that appeared in his native land.

Arenas continued to write while attending the University of Havana. As he began to question Castro's reforms, he was branded as an enemy of the state, expelled from the university, and banned from publishing his work in Cuba. Working as a journalist, Arenas smuggled his fiction out of the country. Several of his books were published in Europe and Latin America to critical acclaim.

In 1973 Arenas was jailed for being a homosexual and a counterrevolutionary. Upon his release three years later, he returned to Havana, where he continued to write while keeping a low profile to evade Cuban officials. After escaping to the United States in 1980, he settled in New York City, where he became one of Castro's most vocal critics. While teaching Cuban literature at several major universities, he wrote fiction and essays, largely focusing on Cuba's history. His only work set in the United States was *El Portero,* which was translated into English under the title *The Doorman.*

Suffering from AIDS, Arenas committed suicide on December 7, 1990. He left behind a note, blaming his suicide on Castro. Published after his death, his memoirs, *Antes que Anochezca* (Before Night Falls), further attacked Castro as an enemy to Cuban artists and writers.

---

homeland. Among their ranks were many of Cuba's finest artists, including poet Reinaldo Arenas, writer Carlos Victoria, painters Juan Abréu and Victor Gómez, and dancer Juanita Baró. Their presence breathed new life into the arts of the Miami area. During the 1980s, Little Havana saw the establishment of hundreds of new theater groups, galleries, publishers, cultural festivals, and arts organizations. This wave of creativity not only revived interest among the exiles in the works of Cuban American artists, both old and new; it also helped combat the negative publicity that had initially haunted the Mariel immigrants. In fact, some artists took to calling themselves Marielitos with pride. Once regarded as an insult, the term had become a badge of honor, identifying them with the most vibrant and innovative aspects of contemporary Cuban American life.

CHAPTER SEVEN

Elian and Beyond

By the late 1980s Cuba was experiencing a new economic crisis. The country had long depended on aid from the Soviet Union, its large and once powerful communist ally. But as the Soviet Union's own economy began to falter, it could no longer afford to send billions of rubles to Cuba each year. Matters grew even worse for Cuba when the Soviet Union dissolved itself in 1991. With no aid at all from this former superpower, the island's economy went into a tailspin. Suddenly, Cubans had no gas for their cars and had to cope with the worst shortages ever of food and other necessities.

Cuban Americans greeted the economic crisis in Cuba with enthusiasm. Although they sympathized with the difficulties average Cubans now faced, they were thrilled to see Castro's revolution unveiled as a failure. No longer propped up by the Soviet Union, Castro, they believed, was sure to fall.

New hopes for a Cuba without Castro galvanized Cuban American politics. Political groups gathered to debate ways they could improve conditions in Cuba both now and in the future. A few organizations, such as the Cuban Democratic Platform, believed in a moderate approach. They held that Castro had become so weak that, with pressure from other countries, he could be persuaded to enact reforms to make his government more democratic.

Most Cuban Americans, however, still preferred a tougher stance. They concentrated their efforts on getting Castro out of power altogether. Rallying around the Cuban American National Foundation (CANF), the most powerful Cuban American political organization, they lobbied U.S. policy makers to tighten the trade embargo that had been in place since 1962. In the short term, Cuban Americans knew this would add to Cubans' misery. But the CANF and its supporters believed it was the best way to push the Cuban people to finally remove Castro from power.

Desperation on the Island

During the early 1990s Castro allowed a few thousand Cubans to emigrate to the United States each year. But most Cubans were unable to obtain legal exit permits or to afford the airfare to America. The only way they could hope to reach the United States was to cross the Straits of Florida by boat. As living conditions grew worse in Cuba, for many the desire to leave became so strong that they were willing to make this dangerous trip in homemade boats and rafts.

Often these immigrants—called *balseros,* or rafters—lost their way and floated aimlessly without food or water for weeks. To save them, sympathetic Cuban Americans founded Brothers to the Rescue in 1991.

Cuban American National Foundation

Perhaps the most powerful force in Cuban American politics, the Cuban American National Foundation (CANF) was founded in 1981 by a group of prominent businesspeople. Led by millionaire Jorge Mas Canosa, CANF was dedicated to restoring democracy to Cuba. As a symbol of its intention to influence national policy, the organization established its headquarters in Washington, D.C., rather than in Miami. As Mas Canosa explained, "We had to take the fight out of Calle Ocho and Miami Stadium and into the center of power. We had to stop the commando raids and concentrate on influencing public opinion and governments."

With hefty financial support from the Cuban American business community, CANF has helped guide U.S. policy toward Cuba. Largely because of CANF's lobbying efforts, the U.S. government established Radio Martí and Television Martí. These stations, based in Florida, broadcast international news to Cuba, whose citizens otherwise would not have access to this information. CANF has also worked to persuade the United States to strengthen its trade embargo with Cuba. More recently, it has vigorously opposed the U.S. policy of returning to Cuba refugees trying to escape to the United States by crossing the Straits of Florida on boats and rafts.

In the past, Cubans who arrived in the United States on rafts were generally allowed to stay in the country, even though technically they had entered the country illegally. Speaking out against this policy, Castro threatened that

> If the U.S. does not take rapid, effective measures to stop promoting illegal departures from [our] country, we will feel obliged to instruct our border guards to do nothing to stop any vessel that is trying to leave Cuba. We have set forth our position; we aren't opposed to solutions if they are based on sincerity and honesty, if they seek to solve the problem, if they aren't proffered as a means of deceiving us—but we cannot continue to act as border guards for the U.S.[63]

As conditions worsened in Cuba, U.S. president Bill Clinton feared another mass migration like the Mariel boatlift of the 1980s, which had been a political disaster for then president Jimmy Carter. To prevent a similar situation, the Clinton administration developed a plan called Operation Distant Shore. If a new flood of immigrants headed by boat for the United States, this time they would be met by U.S. warships determined to block their way.

Many balseros, *or "rafters," have to be rescued by the U.S. Coast Guard or Navy because they lose their way or hit storms in an unforgiving ocean.*

This volunteer organization searched the waters by helicopter. When the volunteers found stranded *balseros,* they tossed food and water to the rafters and called on the U.S. Coast Guard to rescue them.

Opening Immigration

Events in Cuba soon tested America's new policies. In August 1994 several incidents occurred in which Cubans hijacked ferries operating off the coast of Havana and forced the ferry operators to take them to the United States. As word of the hijackings spread in Cuba, crowds of people gathered along the waterfront, hoping to hitch a ride north on the next commandeered ferry. When Castro sent his police to the scene on August 5, a riot erupted. In a huge, spontaneous demonstration, people attacked the police and shouted slogans denouncing Castro's regime.

Castro responded to this crisis as he had to others in the past, saying that any Cubans unhappy with his rule could leave. His aim was twofold. The policy was designed to rid the country of militant discontented Cubans most likely to organize a revolt. Castro also knew the United States did not want another Mariel-style migration. He hoped that by threatening to unleash another wave of immigrants, he could force Clinton to lift the U.S. trade embargo.

Refusing to take Castro's bait, the Clinton administration firmly stated it would not lift the embargo. It also vowed to form a blockade to prevent Cuban Americans from traveling to Cuba to pick up friends and relatives. This time, the only way Cubans would be able to leave the island was aboard their own boats.

The *Balsero* Migration

Within days, tens of thousands of Cubans headed for the beach in spite of indications that they would not be welcome in America. Soon, the Straits of Florida was filled with crude boats and rafts made from anything that would float. Some people tried to cross the ninety-mile-wide waterway with nothing but an inner tube or a plank of wood nailed to a piece of Styrofoam. The cost of these materials soon became so high that would-be rafters often had to sell everything they owned to afford them. A more substantial homemade raft made from oil drums and a cloth sail cost as much as $3,000.

Many of these makeshift rafts sank, stranding and drowning countless people. Even when *balseros'* vessels stayed afloat, they faced many other dangers. Some became delirious and died from dehydration after spending many days baking under the hot Caribbean sun. Others were killed in shark attacks or lost their lives when other desperate *balseros* pirated their rafts. Waves as high as fifteen feet threatened to topple even the most sturdy boats. One *balsero* explained that the waves forced him and his fellow rafters to turn back after traveling nine miles out into the water. "A big wave washed over us, and we all had to hold on for our lives," he said. "Out there nobody is around to help you. You stay afloat or you die."[64]

Alarmed by the futility of their rescue efforts, Arnaldo Iglesias, the leader of Brothers to the Rescue, told the press: "It is total chaos out there, and it's getting worse. We are begging people, 'Please don't do it.'"[65] But despite the warnings and risks, more *balseros* took to the water. Desperate to stop the emigration, Clinton announced that any *balseros* picked up by the U.S. Coast Guard would be placed in detainment camps. About thirty thousand were taken to the navy base that the United States still leased from the Cuban government at Guantanamo Bay. Several thousand more were transported to a U.S. airbase in Panama. President Clinton held

President Clinton ordered that all balseros *picked up by the Coast Guard were to be placed in detainment camps, like the one shown.*

that the *balseros* would be detained until their settlement in another country could be arranged, but under no circumstances would they be allowed to enter the United States.

Life in the Camps

Immediately, the U.S. government scrambled to build tent cities for the detainees. The facilities at Guantanamo Bay alone cost about $1 million a day to operate. More than six thousand U.S. soldiers were placed in charge of the Cubans there. To help the detainees pass the time, they organized baseball and soccer leagues, built libraries, and established schools for both adults and children. But these efforts did little to relieve the tension felt by the Cubans as they waited to hear what their fate would be.

As they languished in the camps, the United States and Cuba entered into negotiations over the fate of the *balseros*. In September 1994 the two countries reached an agreement. Cuba would end the *balsero* migration if the United States agreed to allow a minimum of twenty thousand Cuban legal immigrants to enter the country each year. The detainees could apply for one of these twenty thousand available exit visas only if they first returned to Cuba. To many of the *balseros,* the deal smacked of betrayal. Ramon Quintano, a twenty-five-year-old Cuban detained in Panama, voiced their frustration: "People are very, very hurt and upset with Clinton. We thought we could have a new life. It seems like Clinton and Castro are working together."[66]

With no end of their detention in sight, many Cubans in the tent cities became increasingly desperate. Giving up hope of ever leaving Cuba, about one thousand at Guantanamo Bay escaped from the camp and returned home. Some women became pregnant in hopes that U.S. authorities would send them to Miami for medical care. A few detainees even attempted suicide. The Cubans in Panama were relocated to Guantanamo Bay in February 1995, after they rioted and burned down much of their camp.

Shifting Policies

As summer approached, many U.S. officials feared that the added misery caused by hot weather would lead to riots at Guantanamo Bay as well. Desperate to resolve the issue of what to do with the detainees, the Clinton administration decided in May 1995 to reverse its earlier stance. It agreed to allow most of the Cubans still held at Guantanamo Bay to enter the United States. The same month, however, the government announced that it would end its long-standing policy of giving special consideration to Cuban immigrants in granting them legal residency in the United States. Any Cubans who came to the United States illegally would be deported to Cuba. CANF and other anti-Castro groups condemned Clinton for this action, even going so far as calling him "Fidel Castro's accomplice."[67]

Just as some Cuban Americans feared Clinton was becoming too soft in his dealings with Castro, U.S.-Cuban relations again shifted abruptly. On February 24, 1996, two unarmed airplanes flown by Brothers to the Rescue volunteers were shot down on Castro's orders. Four Cuban Americans lost their lives in the incident.

The incident forced the U.S. government to take a hard line against Cuba. Clinton denounced Castro's actions and threw his support to the 1996 Helms-Burton Bill. Signed into law as the Cuban Liberty and Democratic Solidarity Act, the legislation further tightened the embargo. Further bolstering the anti-Castro faction in the Cuban American community was the 1996 election of Joseph Carollo, a vocal opponent of Castro's, as mayor of Miami. The anti-Castro faction also was assured continuing influence in Washington through the work of Ileana Ros-Lehtinen and Lincoln Diaz-Balart, the two Cuban American members of the U.S. House of Representatives.

Changing Times

This faction, however, soon experienced a series of setbacks. In November 1997 the founder of CANF died suddenly, leaving this powerful anti-Castro organization without a strong leader. Three months later, Pope John Paul II made his first visit to

Cuba. By greeting the leader of the Catholic Church, Castro gave Cuban Americans hope that he might end his repressive policies against organized religion and perhaps make other democratic reforms as well. During his visit, the pope also criticized the U.S. embargo as "morally unethical."[68] This statement provided politically moderate Cuban Americans with another reason to support more open trade between the United States and Cuba.

To these Cuban Americans, the extreme stance of the anti-Castro faction started to seem old-fashioned and unrealistic. They did not see the embargo as doing anything other than making their relatives on the island suffer. Cuban American journalist Arturo Vilar was one of these moderates who expressed doubts about the U.S. trade policies:

> When I travel to Cuba, and I run into people who need everything, I just can't justify continuing the sanctions, let alone tightening them. . . . These days, knowing how hard things have become in Cuba, I have started to have a rough time enjoying all the things that I have here in Miami. It's not so bad when I'm alone, but when I'm with a group of people, at dinner,

During his visit to Cuba in 1998, Pope John Paul II criticized the United States for its embargo on Cuba.

say, . . . I look at the table and I imagine the bare tables of friends in [the Cuban town of] Miramar. We should be sharing our bounty with them, not pressuring the U.S. government to take away what little they have.[69]

Even strong opponents to Castro shared Vilar's concerns. While publicly supporting the embargo, many Cuban American exiles were sending money and goods to their relatives in Cuba. By the late 1990s these gifts poured as much as $1 billion a year into Cuba's ailing economy.

Others also began denouncing the embargo. American businessmen wanted to sell their goods in the Cuban market, while American tourists wanted to vacation on Cuba's unspoiled beaches. Within Cuba, many activists also spoke out against U.S. trade policy and Cuban American support of it. One leader of dissidents living in Cuba, Elizardo Sanchez, claimed that "the belligerent actions of the hard-line exiles in Miami simply keep giving Castro an excuse to crack down on us."[70] Facing opposition from all directions, the influence of the passionately anti-Castro exiles both inside and outside the Cuban American community appeared to be on the wane.

The Elian Gonzalez Controversy

Events, however, continued to keep relations between Cuba, the U.S. government, and the Cuban American community in flux. The most dramatic episode in recent Cuban American history began on November 25, 1999, when fishermen discovered a

Cuban Americans gather in support of Elian Gonzalez staying in the United States.

disoriented five-year-old boy, his arms wrapped around an inner tube, floating in the water three miles off the Florida coast. His name was Elian Gonzalez. Three days before, he and his mother had escaped from Cuba and set off with twelve other Cubans, bound for the United States in a seventeen-foot motorboat. The boat had capsized, and Elian was the only survivor. After a brief stay in a hospital, Elian was released to the custody of his great-uncle, Lazaro, an auto mechanic who lived in the Miami suburb of Hialeah. Although Elian's father Juan immediately asked for the boy to be returned to him in Cuba, his Miami relatives launched a legal battle to keep him in the United States.

The story of Elian soon captured the imagination of the Cuban American community. Many felt sympathy both for the boy and for his mother, who had lost her

Just before dawn on April 22, 2000, armed INS agents took Elian Gonzalez from his uncle's home in Miami.

life trying to bring him to the United States. Leaders in the extreme anti-Castro faction also saw an opportunity to restore their influence by uniting Cuban Americans in a campaign to force the government to let Elian remain in the United States.

The incident worked against the anti-Castro faction, however. Although they hoped to elicit support from non–Cuban Americans, many outside the immigrant community did not understand the exiles' strong feelings against Castro. The majority of Americans simply believed the boy belonged with his father and that politics were irrelevant.

The anti-Castro faction in the Cuban American community also assumed that the Elian Gonzalez controversy would shine a light on U.S.-Cuban relations and perhaps even lead to greater public support for the U.S. trade embargo. But to their dismay, many Americans concluded that the embargo against communist Cuba made little sense. After all, they reasoned, the United States had trade relations with China and Vietnam, which also had repressive communist governments. Contrary to the conservative exiles' hopes, scrutiny of the embargo led more Americans to question its worth. In 1998, 60 percent of Americans were in favor of the embargo. Two years later, during the height of the Elian controversy, only 47 percent thought it was a sound policy.

Just before dawn on April 22, 2000—almost five months after Elian's rescue—armed Immigration and Naturalization Service (INS) agents took the boy from Lazaro Gonzalez's house. Two months later, Elian was returned to Cuba.

The shock waves from the raid reverberated through Miami, but ironically left the Cuban American community in a strengthened position politically. Miami Mayor Joseph Carollo, a highly vocal supporter of Elian's right to stay in the United States, responded with anger toward other city officials. He fired City Manager Donald Warshaw when Warshaw refused to dismiss Police Chief William O'Brien, who neglected to warn Carollo of the INS raid. O'Brien subsequently resigned. The posts of city

Ileana Ros-Lehtinen

In 1989 Ileana Ros-Lehtinen became the first Cuban American and the first Hispanic woman elected to the U.S. Congress. Born Ileana Ros in Havana on July 15, 1952, she moved with her family to Miami in 1960 after Fidel Castro took control of the Cuban government. After receiving a bachelor's and master's degree from Florida International University, she founded Eastern Academy, a private elementary school in southern Florida.

With the encouragement of her father, Ros entered politics in 1982. She was elected to the Florida legislature, where she served for seven years. During this period, Ros met and married fellow legislator Dexter Lehtinen. When longtime congressman Claude D. Pepper died suddenly in 1989, Ileana Ros-Lehtinen left the Florida legislature to run as a Republican for his seat.

The campaign, which pitted her against a non-Cuban, Democrat Gerald F. Richman, was ethnically charged. Because the congressional district was more than 50 percent Hispanic, some suggested that the position should rightfully go to a Hispanic candidate. Richman replied by saying, "This is an American seat," a comment that angered many Cuban Americans because it suggested they were somehow less than full Americans. Cuban Americans turned out in large numbers, allowing Ros-Lehtinen to win with 53 percent of the entire vote. An article published on August 31, 1989, in the *New York Times* called her election "a turning point in the ethnic balance of power in the Miami area."

Ros-Lehtinen has served six terms, often running unopposed in her reelection bids. Throughout her tenure in Congress, she has been a powerful influence on U.S. policy regarding Cuba. Her strong anti-Castro views led *Granma,* a state-run Cuban newspaper, to condemn her as a "ferocious wolf disguised as a woman" in 1999. Eager to take on Castro, she stated in a *New York Times* interview published on January 20, 2000, that the insult made her "pleased as punch," adding "I've been trying for so many years to get him to pick on me."

manager and police chief were then filled by Carlos Gimenez and Raul Martinez, respectively—both Cuban Americans. Three of Miami's five city commissioners were also Cuban Americans.

Despite their increased local political clout, many Cuban Americans still felt defeated and angry following the Elian Gonzalez controversy. Some, like Anna Bonnin, focused their wrath on the U.S. government; as Bonnin explained, "A lot of us have lost our trust in the American way, the American system."[71] Others felt let down by the American people. The case had made clear that Americans no longer supported the stridently anticommunist views of many Cuban Americans. Like it or not, many Cuban Americans had to face that their political views were now far outside the American mainstream.

Two Cubas

April 2001 saw two painful anniversaries for Cuban Americans. One year earlier, Elian Gonzalez had been seized from his Miami relatives' home, effectively ending their struggle to keep him in the United States. Forty years earlier, the members of Brigade 2506 had failed in their attempt to overthrow Castro, dashing the exiles' hopes for a quick return to Cuba. Both incidents remained fresh in the minds of many Cuban Americans. They stood as symbols of their five-decade struggle to reclaim their homeland—a fight many older Cuban Americans began to believe they would not live long enough to win.

The original exiles' dream of driving Castro out by force indeed seems unlikely to come true. However, with Castro well into his seventies, his control on Cuba's government will probably not last much longer. Castro speaks confidently that Cuba's communist regime will live on after his death, stating "No one has the power in this country to change its course."[72] But many Cuban Americans believe that, without Castro in power, Cubans in time will be able to push for reforms, leading to a freer, more democratic Cuba.

Visitors come to see the Bay of Pigs memorial in Miami, Florida.

Gloria Estefan

A superstar since the 1980s, Gloria Estefan has helped introduce Latin rhythms into American pop music. She was born Gloria Fajardo on September 1, 1958, in Cuba. There, her father worked as a bodyguard for the family of the former president Fulgencio Batista. When Batista was ousted from power the following year, the Fajardos fled to Miami. Gloria spent much of her youth caring for her sister and her father, victims of multiple sclerosis, while her mother worked.

Though painfully shy, in her teens she joined a local band, the Miami Latin Boys, while attending the University of Miami. After graduating, she married band leader Emilio Estefan. Renaming the band the Miami Sound Machine, Emilio secured a contract with CBS Records. The group recorded four successful Spanish-language albums, but did not have mainstream success until it began writing and performing songs in English. The Miami Sound Machine's first hit, "Conga," made its way onto the pop, dance, black, and Latin charts. The band also had success with other dance songs with a Latin beat, including "Bad Boys," "Rhythm Is Gonna Get You," and "1-2-3." After these successes, Gloria Estefan began branching out by singing ballads, which became as popular as her dance tunes.

As a solo artist, Estefan has explored her Cuban roots in her acclaimed Spanish-language albums *Mi Tierra, Abriendo Puertas,* and *Alma Caribeña.* In 1994 she

Cuban American superstar Gloria Estefan performs in both Spanish and English.

became the first artist to sing a song in Spanish at the Grammy Awards. Six years later, she was a cohost of the first Latin Grammy Awards in Los Angeles.

With her phenomenal success, Estefan has emerged as a high-profile representative of the Cuban American community. Unafraid of taking a controversial stance, she has helped Cuban-based artists perform in Miami, despite the opposition of many Cuban Americans. Amidst criticism, she also visited the Miami relatives of Elian Gonzalez to show her support for their cause. Despite her outspokenness, Estefan is considered a heroine to many Cuban Americans. Still a resident of Miami, she is affectionately known in her hometown as "nuestra Glorita"—our Gloria.

With these changes, some younger Cuban Americans see opportunity. Just as earlier generations recreated old Havana on American soil, they envision one day investing their time, money, and energy to transform Cuba back into the vibrant, prosperous country it once was. Expressing the optimism many have about post-Castro Cuba, Carlos Alberto Montaner, founder of the political organization Plataforma Democratica Cubana (Cuban Democratic Platform) predicts that Cuban Americans

> will play a very important role in a future Cuba. From an economic perspective, if there is peace and calm in the post-Castro era, Cuban Americans will be constantly traveling and creating a second residence in the island. Gradually, they will develop economic links between the U.S. and Cuba, and Miami will emerge as somewhat of a Cuban city—second only to Havana.[73]

Even though their parents and grandparents lost their country with Castro's coup, younger Cuban Americans have reason to hope that one day they will have two Cubas—one in Miami and one on the island—to call their home.

Notes

Introduction: The Cuban American Success Story
1. Quoted in David Rieff, *The Exile: Cuba in the Heart of Miami.* New York: Simon & Schuster, 1993, p. 31.
2. Miguel Gonzalez-Pando, *The Cuban Americans.* Westport, CT: Greenwood Press, 1998, p. ix.

Chapter One: Between Two Worlds
3. Quoted in James S. Olson and Judith E. Olson, *Cuban Americans: From Trauma to Triumph.* New York: Twayne, 1995, p. 2.
4. Quoted in Louis A. Pérez Jr., *On Becoming Cuban: Indentity, Nationality, & Culture.* Chapel Hill: University of North Carolina Press, 1999, p. 98.
5. Quoted in Leslie Bethell, ed., *Cuba: A Short History.* New York: Cambridge University Press, 1993, p. 38.
6. Quoted in Olson and Olson, *Cuban Americans,* p. 33.

Chapter Two: Escaping Castro
7. Quoted in Beatrice Rodriguez Owsley, *The Hispanic-American Entrepreneur: An Oral History of the American Dream.* New York: Twayne, 1992, p. 30.
8. Quoted in Lynn Geldof, *Cubans: Voices of Change.* New York: St. Martin's Press, 1992, p. 195.
9. Quoted in Barbara Karkabi, "After the Exodus: Four Decades Later, Grown Participants of Operation Pedro Pan Reflect on Their Fateful Flights from Cuba," *Houston Chronicle,* August 1, 1999, p. 1.
10. Pablo Medina, *Exiled Memories: A Cuban Childhood.* Austin: University of Texas Press, 1990, p. 110.
11. Quoted in Joan Morrison and Charlotte Fox Zabusky, *American Mosaic: The Immigrant Experience in the Words of Those Who Lived It.* Pittsburgh: University of Pittsburgh Press, 1993, pp. 324–25.
12. Quoted in Thomas M. Leonard, *Castro and the Cuban Revolution.* Westport, CT: Greenwood Press, 1999, p. 35.
13. Quoted in Terry Dolan, Janet Satterfield, and Chris Stade, eds., *A Road Well Traveled: Three Generations of Cuban American Women.* Newton, MA: Women's Educational Equity Act Program, 1988, p. 66.
14. Quoted in Morrison and Zabusky, *American Mosaic,* p. 321.
15. Quoted in Gonzalez-Pando, *The Cuban Americans,* p. 33.
16. Quoted in Morrison and Zabusky, *American Mosaic,* p. 320.
17. Quoted in María Christina García, *Havana USA: Cuban Exiles and Cuban Americans in South Florida, 1959–1994.* Berkeley: University of California Press, 1996, p. 17.
18. Quoted in García, *Havana USA,* p. 17.
19. Quoted in García, *Havana USA,* p. 17.

Chapter Three: The Golden Exiles
20. Gustavo Pérez Firmat, *Next Year in Cuba: A Cubano's Coming-of-Age in*

America. New York: Doubleday, 1995, p. 65.
21. Quoted in June Namais, *First Generation: In the Words of Twentieth-Century Immigrants*. Boston: Beacon Press, 1978, p. 159.
22. Quoted in García, *Havana USA*, p. 27.
23. Quoted in Karkabi, "After the Exodus," p. 1.
24. Quoted in García, *Havana USA*, p. 33.
25. Quoted in Gonzalez-Pando, *The Cuban Americans*, p. 37.
26. Quoted in Gonzalez-Pando, *The Cuban Americans*, p. 25.
27. Quoted in Gonzalez-Pando, *The Cuban Americans*, p. 26.
28. Quoted in Gonzalez-Pando, *The Cuban Americans*, p. 26.
29. Quoted in José Llanes, *Cuban Americans: Masters of Survival*. Cambridge, MA: Abt Books, 1982, pp. 64–65.
30. Quoted in Olson and Olson, *Cuban Americans*, p. 58.
31. Quoted in García, *Havana USA*, p. 34.

Chapter Four: Blending Old and New

32. Quoted in Gonzalez-Pando, *The Cuban Americans*, p. 39.
33. Quoted in Dolan et al., *A Road Well Traveled*, p. 77.
34. Quoted in García, *Havana USA*, p. 37.
35. Medina, *Exiled Memories*, p. 2.
36. Quoted in Dolan et al., *A Road Well Traveled*, p. 77.
37. Quoted in Evelyn Nieves, "Union City and Miami," *New York Times*, November 30, 1992, p. B1.
38. Quoted in Gonzalez-Pando, *The Cuban Americans*, p. 134.
39. Firmat, *Next Year in Cuba*, p. 80.
40. Quoted in Gonzalez-Pando, *The Cuban Americans*, p. 87.
41. Firmat, *Next Year in Cuba*, p. 73.
42. Quoted in García, *Havana USA*, p. 38.

Chapter Five: Becoming Cuban American

43. Quoted in Geldof, *Cubans*, pp. 215–16.
44. Quoted in Rieff, *The Exile*, p. 134.
45. Quoted in Robert M. Levine and Moisés Asis, *Cuban Miami*. New Brunswick, NJ: Rutgers University Press, 2000, pp. 78–79.
46. Quoted in Dolan et al., *A Road Well Traveled*, p. 116.
47. Quoted in García, *Havana USA*, p. 144.
48. Quoted in Geldof, *Cubans*, p. 248.
49. Quoted in García, *Havana USA*, p. 27.
50. Quoted in Dolan, et al., *A Road Well Traveled*, p. 118.
51. Mirta Ojito, "'You Are Going to El Norte,'" *New York Times Magazine*, April 23, 2000, p. 6.
52. Quoted in Olson and Olson, *Cuban Americans*, p. 80.

Chapter Six: The Marielitos

53. Quoted in Llanes, *Cuban Americans*, p. 150.
54. Quoted in Llanes, *Cuban Americans*, p. 151.
55. Quoted in García, *Havana USA*, p. 59.
56. Gonzalez-Pando, *The Cuban Americans*, p. 66.
57. Ojito, "'You Are Going to El Norte,'" p. 6.
58. Quoted in García, *Havana USA*, p. 61.
59. Quoted in Levine, *Cuban Miami*, p. 47.
60. Ojito, "'You Are Going to El Norte,'" p. 6.
61. Quoted in Llanes, *Cuban Americans*, pp. 182–83.

62. Quoted in Marie Arana-Ward, "Three Marielitos, Three Manifest Destinies," *Washington Post,* July 9, 1996, p. A1.

Chapter Seven: Elian and Beyond

63. Quoted in Larry Nackerud et al., "The End of the Cuban Contradiction in U.S. Refugee Policy," *International Migration Review,* Spring 1999, p. 33.
64. Quoted in Tod Robberson, "Cubans Still Pin Hopes on Flimsy Rafts," *Washington Post,* September 6, 1994, p. A10.
65. Quoted in Frances Robles and Martin Merzer, "Cubans Risk Lives on 'Anything That Floats,'" *Houston Chronicle,* August 23, 1994, p. 1.
66. Quoted in Douglas Farah, "U.S. Begins Flying Cuban Refugees in Panama to Guantanamo Naval Base," *Washington Post,* February 2, 1995, p. A18.
67. Quoted in Peter Kornbluh, "Cuba No Mas," *The Nation,* May 29, 1995, p. 745.
68. Quoted in Carla Anne Robbins, "Idea of Limited Aid for Cuba Gains Respectability as Exiles, Legislators, Lobbyists Fight over Form," *Wall Street Journal,* April 15, 1998, p. A24.
69. Quoted in Rieff, *The Exile,* p. 169.
70. Quoted in Tim Padgett, "Out with the Old?" *Time,* April 17, 2000, p. 32.
71. Quoted in John-Thor Dahlburg, "Cuban Americans Still Angry over Elian." *Los Angeles Times,* April 23, 2001, p. A10.
72. Quoted in Laurie Goering, "The Revolution Will Live Beyond Me, Castro Says," *Chicago Tribune,* March 18, 2001, p. 1.
73. Quoted in Gonzalez-Pando, *The Cuban Americans,* p. 164.

For Further Reading

Books

Todd M. Appel, *Jose Marti*. New York: Chelsea House, 1992. Young adult biography of the nineteenth-century Cuban revolutionary.

Alma Flor Ada, *Where the Flame Trees Bloom*. New York: Atheneum, 1994. Memoir featuring eleven stories about the author's childhood in Cuba.

Susan Garver and Paula McGuire, *Coming to North America from Mexico, Cuba, and Puerto Rico*. New York: Delacorte, 1981. Covers the experiences of Cuban immigrants, as well as those of other Hispanic American ethnic groups.

Kathlyn Gay, *Leaving Cuba: From Operation Pedro Pan to Elian*. Brookfield, CT: Twenty-First Century Books, 2000. Historical survey of Cuban immigration to the United States, including an overview of the Elian Gonzalez controversy.

Renée Gernand, *The Cuban Americans*. New York: Chelsea House, 1996. Young adult history of Cuban immigration to the United States.

James Haskins, *The New Americans: Cuban Boat People*. Hillside, NJ: Enslow, 1982. Account of the Marielito boatlift and the experiences of Marielitos in the United States.

Dorothy Hoobler and Thomas Hoobler, *The Cuban American Family Album*. New York: Oxford University Press, 1996. Collection of first-person narratives by Cuban Americans on such subjects as school, family, and religion.

Adriana Mendez Rodenas, *Cubans in America*. Minneapolis, MN: Lerner, 1994. Description of the culture and politics of the Cuban American community.

Websites

Facts About Cuban Exiles (www.cubaface.org) Offers information about the contributions of Cuban Americans to American society.

generation ñ (generation-n.citysearch.com) Web version of a magazine edited by Cuban American Bill Teck that discusses issues of concern for young Hispanic Americans.

Operation Pedro Pan Group (www.pedropan.org) Site created by a nonprofit organization dedicated to documenting the history of the Cuban children who came to the United States on the Pedro Pan flights in the early 1960s.

Works Consulted

Books

Leslie Bethell, ed., *Cuba: A Short History.* New York: Cambridge University Press, 1993. Brief historical survey of Cuba from 1750 to the early 1990s.

Thomas D. Boswell and James R. Curtis, *The Cuban-American Experience: Culture, Images, and Perspectives.* Totowa, NJ: Rowman & Allanheld, 1984. Useful study of Cuban American society, including discussions of demographics, language, religion, cuisine, politics, and the arts.

Terry Dolan, Janet Satterfield, and Chris Stade, eds., *A Road Well Traveled: Three Generations of Cuban American Women.* Newton, MA: Women's Educational Equity Act Program, 1988. Exploration of the role of women in Cuban American society.

Flor Ferandez Barrios, *Blessed by Thunder: Memoirs of a Cuban Girlhood.* Seattle: Seal Press, 1999. A memoir of the author's experiences of growing up in Castro's Cuba and remaking her life in the United States in the 1970s.

María Christina García, *Havana USA: Cuban Exiles and Cuban Americans in South Florida, 1959–1994.* Berkeley: University of California Press, 1996. Lively history of the formation of the Cuban American community in south Florida.

Lynn Geldof, *Cubans: Voices of Change.* New York: St. Martin's Press, 1992. Collection of interviews with Cubans and Cuban Americans, representing a wide range of backgrounds and experiences.

Miguel Gonzalez-Pando, *The Cuban Americans.* Westport, CT: Greenwood Press, 1998. Balanced account of the Cuban immigrant experience written by the founder of the Cuban Living History Project at Florida International University.

Alfredo Jiménez, ed., *Handbook of Hispanic Cultures in the United States,* vol. 2. Houston, TX: Arte Público Press, 1993. Includes a lengthy article on Cubans in the United States.

Thomas M. Leonard, *Castro and the Cuban Revolution.* Westport, CT: Greenwood Press, 1999. Provides an overview of factors leading to Castro's rise to power and includes a chapter on Cuban American exiles.

Robert M. Levine and Moisés Asis, *Cuban Miami.* New Brunswick, NJ: Rutgers University Press, 2000. Brief history of Cuban Americans in Miami with many well-chosen photographs.

José Llanes, *Cuban Americans: Masters of Survival.* Cambridge, MA: Abt Books, 1982. Includes extensive selections from interviews with Cubans who emigrated to the United States between 1959 and 1982.

Pablo Medina, *Exiled Memories: A Cuban Childhood.* Austin: University of Texas Press, 1990. Memoir of the author's youth in Cuba in the 1950s.

Joan Morrison and Charlotte Fox Zabusky, *American Mosaic: The Immigrant Experience in the Words of Those Who Lived It.* Pittsburgh: University of

Pittsburgh Press, 1993. Includes selections from interviews with several Cuban Americans.

June Namais, *First Generation: In the Words of Twentieth-Century Immigrants.* Boston: Beacon Press, 1978. Collection of interviews with immigrants, including some Cuban Americans.

James S. Olson and Judith E. Olson, *Cuban Americans: From Trauma to Triumph.* New York: Twayne, 1995. Solid overview of the history of Cuban American immigration.

Louis A. Pérez Jr., *On Becoming Cuban: Indentity, Nationality, & Culture.* Chapel Hill: University of North Carolina Press, 1999. Cultural history that explores how Cuba's relationship with the United States helped forge the Cuban people's sense of identity.

Gustavo Pérez Firmat, *Next Year in Cuba: A Cubano's Coming-of-Age in America.* New York: Doubleday, 1995. An engaging memoir recounting a Cuban American professor's memories of growing up in Little Havana.

Lorrin Phillipson and Rafael Llerena, *Freedom Flights: Cuban Refugees Talk About Life Under Castro and How They Fled His Regime.* New York: Random House, 1980. Collection of firsthand accounts of Cubans who escaped to the United States during the 1960s and 1970s.

Delia Posey and Virgil Suárez, eds., *Little Havana Blues: A Cuban-American Literature Anthology.* Houston, TX: Arte Público Press, 1996. Excellent anthology of poetry, fiction, plays, and essays by Cuban Americans about their experiences in Cuba and the United States.

David Rieff, *The Exile: Cuba in the Heart of Miami.* New York: Simon & Schuster, 1993. Journalist's portrait of middle-aged Cuban Americans in Miami, focusing on their feelings toward Cuba and the United States.

Beatrice Rodriguez Owsley, *The Hispanic-American Entrepreneur: An Oral History of the American Dream.* New York: Twayne, 1992. Discusses entrepreneurs who have contributed to the economic success of the Cuban American community.

Al Santoli, *New Americans: An Oral History.* New York: Ballantine, 1988. Includes "The Blue-Eyed Cuban," an interview with Pedro Roboredo, a Cuban exile who served as the mayor of West Miami during the 1980s.

María de los Angeles Torres, *In the Land of Mirrors: Cuban Exile Politics in the United States.* Ann Arbor: University of Michigan Press, 1999. Well-researched study of the development of Cuban American politics.

Periodicals

Marie Arana-Ward, "Three Marielitos, Three Manifest Destinies," *Washington Post,* July 9, 1996.

James Cox, "Hungry Eyes Look Toward Cuba as Sun Sets on Castro," *USA Today,* May 10, 2001.

John-Thor Dahlburg, "Cuban Americans Still Angry over Elian," *Los Angeles Times,* April 23, 2001.

Douglas Farah, "U.S. Begins Flying Cuban Refugees in Panama to Guantanamo Naval Base," *Washington Post,* February 2, 1995.

Nancy Gibbs et al., "The Elian Grab," *Time,* May 1, 2000.

Laurie Goering, "The Revolution Will Live Beyond Me, Castro Says," *Chicago Tribune,* March 18, 2001.

Barbara Karkabi, "After the Exodus: Four Decades Later, Grown Participants of Operation Pedro Pan Reflect on Their Fateful Flights from Cuba," *Houston Chronicle,* August 1, 1999.

Francine Kiefer, "Behind Elian Debate, A Faded Fear of Communism," *Christian Science Monitor,* April 27, 2000.

Peter Kornbluh, "Cuba No Mas," *The Nation,* May 29, 1995.

Larry Nackerud et al., "The End of the Cuban Contradiction in U.S. Refugee Policy," *International Migration Review,* Spring 1999.

Evelyn Nieves, "Union City and Miami," *New York Times,* November 30, 1992.

Mirta Ojito, "'You Are Going to El Norte,'" *New York Times Magazine,* April 23, 2000.

Tim Padgett, "Out with the Old?" *Time,* April 17, 2000.

Louis A. Perez, Jr., "Reminiscences of a Lector: Cuban Cigar Workers in Tampa," *Tampa Bay History,* Fall/Winter 1985.

Tod Robberson, "Cubans Still Pin Hopes on Flimsy Rafts," *Washington Post,* September 6, 1994.

Carla Anne Robbins, "Idea of Limited Aid for Cuba Gains Respectability as Exiles, Legislators, Lobbyists Fight over Form," *Wall Street Journal,* April 15, 1998.

Linda Robinson and Jeff Glasser, "A Case of Cuba Fatigue," *U.S. News & World Report,* April 24, 2000.

Frances Robles and Martin Merzer, "Cubans Risk Lives on 'Anything That Floats,'" *Houston Chronicle,* August 23, 1994.

Deborah Sharp, "Exiles Find Comfort in Shrine Facing Homeland," *USA Today,* January 21, 1998.

María de los Angeles Torres, "Elian and the Tale of Pedro Pan," *The Nation,* March 27, 2000.

INDEX

Abdala (Cuban student group), 68
Abréu, Juan, 85
agriculture. *See* Cuba, agriculture of
American Civil Liberties Union, 79
Amorós, Sandy, 31
annexation. *See* Cuba, annexation of
Antes que Anochezca (Arenas), 85
Antonio Maceo Brigade, 70, 71
Areito (magazine), 71
Arenas, Reinaldo, 85
arms embargo, 29
Arnaz, Desi, 31, 35
art, 66–67, 72
assimilation, 10–11, 65–68
athletes, 31

backlash, 83, 84
Baker, James, 40
Ball, Lucille, 35
balseros (boat refugees), 87–91
Baró, Juanita, 85
baseball, 31
Batista, Fulgencio, 26, 28–29
Bay of Pigs invasion, 46–48, 69
Bay of Pigs Museum and Library, 45
Blessed by Thunder: Memoir of a Cuban Girlhood (Fernandez Barrios), 28
blockade, 89
blue jeans revolution, 71–73
boatlift, 59–60, 77–80
boxers, 31
"brain drain," 34–35

Brigade 2506, 45–48, 96
Brigade 2506 Association, 45
Brothers to the Rescue, 87–88, 89, 91
business, 63

Calle Ocho (Eighth Street), 54–55
Camarioca boatlift, 59–60
Campaneris, Bert, 31
camps, 81, 83, 89–91
CANF. *See* Cuban American National Foundation
Carollo, Joseph, 91, 95–96
Carrasco, Teok, 72
Carter, Jimmy, 76, 80
Casal, Lourdes, 71
casinos, 26
Castillo, Siro del, 79
Castro, Fidel
  air flights to Miami and, 49
  anti-American speeches, 44
  Bay of Pigs invasion and, 46–48
  blue jeans revolution and, 73
  Catholic Church and, 91–92
  communism and, 44
  confiscation of land and assets, 44
  denunciation of refugees, 76
  Dialogue Policy, 70–71, 73
  economic policies, 32
  land use policies, 29–30
  name-calling of exiles, 50
  poor Cubans and, 26–27
  ransom for Bay of Pigs invasion prisoners, 48
  recruitment of Cubans in Florida, 27

reform policies, 29
repressive policies, 30–31
Soviet Union and, 40, 44, 49
26th of July Movement and, 26–29
"undesirables" and, 79–80
Catholic Welfare Bureau, 40
Celestina antes del Alba (Arenas), 85
Central Intelligence Agency (CIA), 46, 49
Centro Hispanico Católico (Latin American Catholic Center), 39
Céspedes, Carlos Manuel de, 15–16
Chiriro, Willy, 66
Christmas Eve celebration. *See* Nochebuena
CIA. *See* Central Intelligence Agency
Ciboney (Indian tribe), 13
Cigar City, Florida, 17–19
cigar factories, 17–19
Clinton, Bill, 88, 91
Club de la Habana (The Havana Club), 15
Coalition to Support Cuban Detainees, 79
Columbus, Christopher, 12
Conde, Yvonne M., 42
constitution (Republic of Cuba), 15
corruption, 26
crime rates, 83
criollos, 13–15
CRP. *See* Cuban Refugee Program
Cruz, Celia, 59

Cuba
  agriculture of 13–14
  annexation of, by U.S., 15
  purchase of, by U.S., 15
  return to, 10, 11
Cuban Adjustment Act of 1966, 68–69
Cuban American National Foundation (CANF), 87, 91
Cuban Democratic Platform. *See* Plataforma Democratica Cubana
Cuban Families Committee for the Release of Cuban Prisoners of War, 47–48
Cuban Liberty and Democratic Solidarity Act, 91
Cuban Missile Crisis, 49
Cuban Refugee Committee, 39
Cuban Refugee Emergency Center, 39
Cuban Refugee Program (CRP), 39–40, 51–54, 60–61
Cuban Revolutionary Party. *See* Partido Revolucionario Cubano
Cubelo, José, 31
Cugat, Xavier, 31, 35
culture, 58, 66–67, 71, 84–85, 87, 97
customs, 39, 53–54, 55–59, 65, 72, 82

dancing, 31
Desilu (production company), 35
detainment camps, 89–91
Dialogue Policy, 70–71, 73
Diaz-Balart, Lincoln, 91
Durán, Alfredo, 69

economics, 55–56, 63–64
education, 63–64
Eighth Street. *See* Calle Ocho

Eisenhower, Dwight D., 39
El Caso Padilla (Casal), 71
El Habanero (newspaper), 14
El Portero (Arenas), 85
embargo, 89, 91, 92–93, 94
entrepreneurship, 63
Estefan, Gloria, 97
excludable aliens, 70, 79
Exiled Memories: A Cuban Childhood (Medina), 52
extinction (of indigenous Cubans), 13

Facts About Cuban Exiles (political group), 79
Family Reunification Flights, 60–61, 62
Federation of Cuban Students, 68
Fernandez Barrios, Flor, 28
fifteenth birthday celebration. *See quinceañera*
finance, 63
food, 55, 57, 58
  shortage, 32
Freedom Flights, 60–61, 62

gambling, 26
Golden Exiles, 9–10, 61
Gómez, Máximo, 20, 22
Gómez, Victor, 85
Gonzalez, Elian, 93–96
Gonzalez, Lazaro, 93, 95
Gonzalez-Pando, Miguel, 11, 47, 77
Granma (newspaper), 95
Guanahatabey (Indian tribe), 13
Guantanamo Bay, 89–90, 91
Guatemala, 46
Guillot, Olga, 59

hardships, 77–79, 83–84, 89–91
Hearst, William Randolph, 21
Helms-Burton Bill (1996), 91

Herrera, María Christina, 62–63
Hialeh, Florida, 84
hijacking, 88–89

Iglesias, Arnaldo, 89
I Love Lucy (television program), 35
immigration
  confiscation of property and, 36
  countries other than Cuba, 32–33, 75
  emotional stress, 36
  Florida and, 9, 33, 34, 36
  impact on schools, 39, 40
  Miami and, 37–38, 42–43
  political organizations, 44
  relief for needy in Miami, 39–40
Immigration and Naturalization Service (INS), 81, 95
Indians, 13
INS. *See* Immigration and Naturalization Service
Institute of Cuban Studies, 62, 71
Instituto San Carlos (San Carlos Institute), 16

John Paul II (pope), 91–92
Johnson, Lyndon B., 52, 60

Kennedy, Jacqueline, 48
Kennedy, John F., 39, 47, 48, 49
Key West, Florida, 18, 27, 77
Kid Chocolate, 31
Kid Gavilán, 31

labor unions, 19
land, 30
Lecuona, Ernesto, 31
Little Havana, Florida, 9, 45, 54–59, 61, 63–65
López, Narciso, 15

Maceo, Antonio, 20
Machado, Gerardo, 35
Maine (U.S. warship), 21
Mariel boatlift, 77–80
Marielitos
  hardships, 77–79, 83–84
  Hialeah and, 84
  influence on others, 84–85
  Mariel boatlift, 77–80
  Peruvian Embassy episode, 74–75
  racial/ethnic composition, 82
  statistics, 82
Martí, José, 17, 19–20, 87
Martinez Ybor, Vincente, 18
Mas Canosa, Jorge, 87
McKinley, William, 20–21
Medina, Pablo, 29, 52
Memorandum of Understanding, 60
Miami, Florida, 9–10, 43
Miami Herald (newspaper), 45
Miami Sound Machine (musical group), 97
mobsters, 26
Montaner, Carlos Alberto, 98
municipios (immigrant support organizations), 39
music, 31, 66, 97

Négrin, Eulalio José, 71
networking, 55–56
New York Times (newspaper), 45–46, 53, 79, 95
Next Year in Cuba (Pérez Firmat), 57
Nixon, Richard M., 68
Nochebuena (Christmas Eve celebration), 57, 58

OAS. *See* Organization of American States
Operation Distant Shore, 88
Operation Pedro Pan, 40–43

Operation Pedro Pan: The Untold Exodus of 14,048 Cuban Children (Conde), 42
Organization of American States (OAS), 68
Our Lady of Charity, 72

Panama, 89–90
Partido Revolucionario Cubano (PRC), 19
Pedrosa, Paulina, 17
Pérez, Louis A., Jr., 18
Pérez Firmat, Gustavo, 38, 56–57, 59, 67
Pérez-Franco, Juan E., 45
Peru, 74–75
Plataforma Democratica Cubana (Cuban Democratic Platform), 86–87, 98
Platt Amendment, 22–23
politics
  Antonio Maceo Brigade, 70
  communication (with Cuba), 70–71
  Cuban American involvement, 10–11
  Elian Gonzalez episode, 93–96
  Marielito influence, 84
  municipios, 39
  protests, 68, 79
  trade embargo, 86–87, 92–93
  voting, 68–70
PRC. *See* Partido Revolucionario Cubano
prisoners of war, 47–48
Pulitzer, Joseph, 21
purchase. *See* Cuba, purchase of

quince. See quinceañera
quinceañera (fifteenth birthday celebration), 53

Radio Martí, 87
radio stations, 59
Ramos, Pedro, 31
Reboso, Manolo, 69
religion, 72, 82
repression, 30–31
resettlement, 51–54
returning. *See* Cuba, return to
riots, 77
Rodriguez Santana, Carlos "Carlay," 45
Rojas, Cookie, 31
Roman, Agustin, 72
Ros-Lehtinen, Ileana, 91, 95

Sanchez, Elizardo, 93
Santería, 82
Sierra Maestra (mountain range), 28
Soriano, Rafael, 66–67
Soviet Union, 49, 68, 86
Spanish-American War, 20–23, 24
Spanish colonization, 12–22
Spanish Republic and the Cuban Revolution, The (Martí), 20
statistics
  boatlifts, 77
  Camarioca boatlift, 59
  Cuban immigration to Florida, 9
  early Castro years, 39
  Freedom Flights, 62
  immigration before and after Castro, 8
  Mariel boatlift, 77
  Marielitos, 82
  Operation Pedro Pan, 41
  "undesirables," 81
Straits of Florida, 14, 59–60
Sullivan, Ed, 48

Taino (Indian tribe), 13

Tampa Bay History (magazine), 18
Television Martí, 87
tent cities, 81, 83
Ten Years' War, 15–17
terrorism, 68, 71, 77–78
Thomas, John F., 52
trade, 64
    embargo, 89, 91, 92–93, 94
    partnerships, 14

26th of July Movement, 25–29

Unaccompanied Cuban Children's Program, 40–43
"undesirables," 79–80, 81
unemployment, 83
unions, 19

Varadero, Cuba, 60
Varela, Carlos Muñis, 71
Varela y Morales, Felix, 14

Velázquez, Diego, 13
Victoria, Carlos, 85
voting, 68–71

Walsh, Bryan, 40
women, 64

Ybor City, Florida, 17–19, 27
YUCAs (Young Urban Cuban Americans), 67

Picture Credits

Cover photo: Associated Press
© AFP/CORBIS, 93
© Tony Arruza/CORBIS, 56, 65
© Nathan Benn/CORBIS, 63, 69
© Bettmann/CORBIS, 9, 13, 16, 19, 23, 25, 30, 34, 35, 43, 44, 60, 76, 78
© CORBIS, 15
© John Ficara/Woodfin Camp and Associates, 81
© Chuck Fishman/Woodfin Camp and Associates, 51, 58, 67
© Dave G. Houser/CORBIS, 10
Hulton/Archive by Getty Images, 21, 22, 33, 41, 46, 48
© Catharine Karnow/Woodfin Camp and Associates, 96
Arturo Marti/Vatican/Reuters, 92
Kevin McKiernan/SIPA, 73
© Dan Miller/ Woodfin Camp and Associates, 80, 84
© Rolando Pujol/Woodfin Camp and Associates, 26, 27
© A. Ramey/ Woodfin Camp and Associates, 59
© Olivier Rebbot/Woodfin Camp and Associates, 83
© Reuters NewMedia Inc./CORBIS, 97
Marc Serota/Reuters, 94
SIPA, 75, 88
© Leif Skoogfors/CORBIS, 90
Bob Strong/SIPA, 38
© Patrick Ward/CORBIS, 66
© Nik Wheeler/CORBIS, 54

About the Author

Liz Sonneborn is a writer and an editor who lives in Brooklyn, New York. A graduate of Swarthmore College, she has written more than twenty books for children and adults, including *A to Z of American Women in the Performing Arts*, *The Scholastic History of the American West*, and *The New York Public Library's Amazing Native American History*, winner of a 2000 Parents' Choice Award.